Mermaids

The Myths, Legends, & Lore

SKYE ALEXANDER

adamsmedia
Avon, Massachusetts

Published by
Adams Media, a division of F+W Media, Inc.
57 Littlefield Street, Avon, MA 02322. U.S.A.
www.adamsmedia.com

ISBN 10: 1-4405-3857-3
ISBN 13: 978-1-4405-3857-5
eISBN 10: 1-4405-3855-7
eISBN 13: 978-1-4405-3855-1

Printed in the United States of America.

10   9   8   7   6   5   4   3

Library of Congress Cataloging-in-Publication Data
is available from the publisher.

This publication is designed to provide accurate and authoritative information with regard to the subject matter covered. It is sold with the understanding that the publisher is not engaged in rendering legal, accounting, or other professional advice. If legal advice or other expert assistance is required, the services of a competent professional person should be sought.
　　—From a *Declaration of Principles* jointly adopted by a Committee of the American Bar Association and a Committee of Publishers and Associations

Many of the designations used by manufacturers and sellers to distinguish their product are claimed as trademarks. Where those designations appear in this book and Adams Media was aware of a trademark claim, the designations have been printed with initial capital letters.

Art © Dover Publications;
Title page and Chapter Openers © istockphoto.com/Angelgild

*This book is available at quantity discounts for bulk purchases.
For information, please call 1-800-289-0963.*

DEDICATION

In memory of Don Chandler, fellow writer and friend

ACKNOWLEDGMENTS

I wish to thank the mermaids currently posing as lovely ladies at Adams Media, especially Paula Munier, Andrea Hakanson, and Katie Corcoran Lytle, for making this book possible. I'm also indebted to my supportive sister Myke and my circle of women friends who embody the best qualities of mermaids, and who (so far as I know) haven't drowned a man yet, though I'm sure they've considered it.

Contents

THE *Mermaid Mystique*

> "[H]umans must be much more aware of their surroundings
> if they wish to see these beings. We tend to be aware of the big
> picture and forget to look at the small, lovely details in life."
>
> —D. J. Conway, *Magickal Mermaids and Water Creatures*

ysterious, magical, and mesmerizingly beautiful, mermaids have enchanted humanity for thousands of years. No matter where you go on planet Earth, you'll hear stories of these elusive and evocative sea creatures who are sometimes benevolent, sometimes destructive, but always alluring. They swim in the seven seas; splash about in rivers, lakes, and streams; and even frolic in fountains and wells. And these magical creatures play a more important role in today's society than you may think.

Disney's animated version of Hans Christian Andersen's fairy tale *The Little Mermaid* is one of the biggest box office hits of all time; in its first week, the movie grossed more than $6 million—and that number is now well into the billions. Seventy-five percent of Copenhagen's tourists go to see the Little Mermaid statue. Each year, hundreds of thousands of spectators and exhibitionists crowd the streets of New York's Coney Island to celebrate mermaids in the Coney Island Mermaid Parade. And tens of millions of online sites are dedicated to mermaids. Why are we so fascinated?

Some researchers theorize that we're drawn to the dichotomy of light and dark that mermaids embody. These lovely ladies are simultaneously desirable and dangerous. They can bring good luck or disaster. Seafarers have long swapped stories about mermaids charming sailors with their heavenly singing, then smashing their ships and drowning the hapless seamen. Mermaid myths usually depict these sensuous sirens with a dual nature—they can be benevolent or malevolent, depending on what mood they're in at any given time. Like women, it's a mermaid's prerogative to change her mind—and when she does, watch out!

As you explore the history of mermaids in these pages, read the scores of colorful myths and legends about sea-beings, and chuckle at some of the oddities associated with them, you'll find yourself intrigued by these beguiling beings of the deep. But, as you dive in, be careful. You never know what mysteries are lurking in the fathoms below.

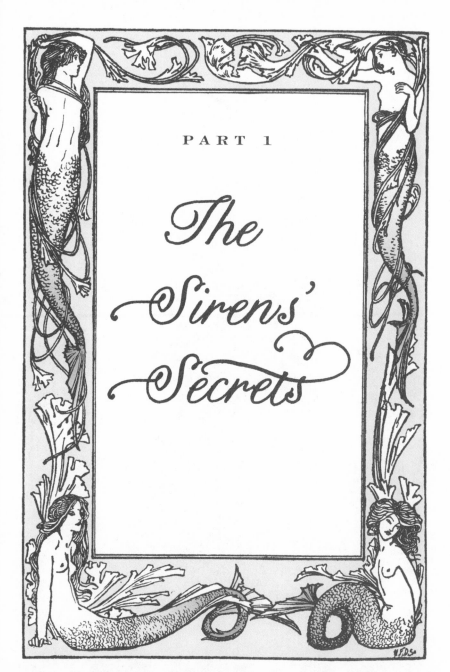

PART 1

The Sirens' Secrets

"Who would be
A mermaid fair,
Singing alone,
Combing her hair
Under the sea,
In a golden curl
With a comb of pearl,
On a throne?
I would be a mermaid fair;
I would sing to myself the whole of the day;
With a comb of pearl I would comb my hair;
And still as I comb I would sing and say,
'Who is it loves me? who loves not me?'"

—Lord Alfred Tennyson, *The Mermaid*

CHAPTER 1

THE *Origins* OF *Mermaids*

MERMAIDS HAVE SPLASHED ABOUT the waters of the world for millennia. But where do these lovely creatures of the sea come from, and how have they captured the imaginations of people around the globe? Here we'll explore the origins of these mysterious aquatic beings, from the streams and rivers of ancient Babylonia to the shining seas of the New World and beyond.

The Symbolism of Water

he sea has long been connected with emotions, intuition, and the unconscious. Deep, dark, and mysterious, the ocean still holds secrets we may never discover. We generally give water a feminine face, associating its changeable nature—its fertility and nourishment, its undulating and sensual rhythms—with women. The ocean's duality mirrors that of mermaids—it brings food, but also devastating storms. So perhaps it's no surprise to find the waters of the world populated by female sea creatures who can protect human beings or destroy them.

Psychoanalysts might explain mermaids as symbols of the male psyche—specifically of a man's unconscious feminine side, or *anima* in Jungian terminology. A man who's out of touch with his inner female might see women as alluring, yet frightening—an image that gets projected onto mermaids. Remember, it's mostly men who see mermaids and it's men whom these awesome beauties usually drown.

Life on Earth cannot survive without water, and our ancestors naturally attributed mystical powers to it. Ancient cultures wor-

shiped powerful water goddesses whom they thought ruled the oceans, lakes, and rivers. In those long-ago times, when the universe was more mysterious and magical than it is today, people believed deities of all kinds controlled virtually every aspect of existence—and water divinities were among the most revered and feared. From these mighty gods and goddesses came the merfolk we know today.

Some early people thought human beings evolved from merfolk—and in a way, perhaps we did. Science tells us that all life originated in the sea, and human embryos develop from fish-like forms in the salty amniotic fluid of their mothers' wombs. Maybe we love mermaids because when we look at them we see reflections of ourselves.

Of the Water Born

 e depend on water for our very existence, so it's no surprise that people have long attributed magical and divine properties to water. The word "mer" comes from the Old English *mere*, meaning sea. In French, the word for sea is *mer* and the word for mother is *mere*, suggesting that the sea is mother to us all.

And as the sea nurtures people from all cultures and walks of life, so, in one form or another, do mermaids appear in virtually all cultures past and present—and their stories are as colorful as the people who tell them.

The ancient Greeks called her sea goddess.

According to the Roman poet Ovid's epic *Metamorphoses*, when the Trojans' ships burned during the Trojan War, their wood transformed into the bodies of sea goddesses—or as Ovid described them, the "green daughters of the sea"—and mermaids were born.

The Celts called her merrow.

Merrow comes from *muir*, meaning "sea," and *oigh*, meaning "maid." An Irish legend says pagan women became mermaids when St. Patrick chased them from the land in the process of converting Ireland from the Old Religion to Christianity.

The Latvians call her nara, and the Estonians call her näkineitsi.

According to the folklore of the indigenous people of Latvia and Estonia, children who were drowned in the Red Sea by the Pharaoh morphed into mermaids.

The question of how mermaids came into being may never be answered—but that, too, is part of their mystery and mystique.

THE MERMAIDS OF NOAH'S ARK

Merfolk even appear in the beloved Bible story of Noah's Ark, according to Christian mythology of the infamous flood. A fifteenth-century illustration from the notable Nuremberg Bible pictures a mermaid, a merman, and even a merdog swimming beside Noah's Ark.

Half-Fish, Half-Human, and All Divine

"Darwin may have been quite correct in his theory that man
descended from the apes of the forest, but surely woman rose from
the frothy sea, as resplendent as Aphrodite on her scalloped chariot."

—Margot Datz, *A Survival Guide for Landlocked Mermaids*

any ancient traditions viewed mermaids as more than
simply enticing sirens of the deep—these beauties
were divine. Water gods and goddesses governed the
oceans, seas, lakes, and rivers of the world. Stories
of these deities have been handed down to us through the ages via
oral tradition, art, and music.

The first recorded story of a mermaid comes to us from Assyria,
circa 1000 B.C.E. Mythology tells us that Atargatis fell in love with
a human being—a young shepherd—as gods and goddesses often
did in those days. Some legends say she accidentally killed him; others say she became pregnant and was shocked when their daughter
was born human. Either way, the distraught goddess threw herself
into a lake. Legend has it that the water could not hide her otherworldly beauty, so she became a mermaid, half-fish, half-human—
and remained divine.

But long before Atargatis, the ancient world honored its water
gods and goddesses. The early Babylonians, for example, credited
the man-fish god Ea (a.k.a. Oannes) with teaching humankind agriculture, architecture, and much more. The Phoenicians worshiped a
half-fish, half-man god named Dagon. According to the Aborigines,
life-giving spirits called yawkyawks, who looked like women with

fishtails, resided in Australia's sacred water holes. Ancient Greek and Roman art depicts water deities with bodies that combined the traits of humans and aquatic creatures, the most famous being the god Triton, son of the sea rulers Poseidon and Amphitrite.

Merfolk quite likely derived from these ancient divinities. Though less formidable than Ea, Dagon, Poseidon, and Amphitrite, mermaids and mermen possessed their own powers—from bestowing good luck on humans to brewing up ferocious storms at sea. Merfolk could be compassionate or malevolent—and might just as well destroy people as rescue them.

OF SHELLS AND CONCHES

Triton served as the "model" for the famous marble Fountain of Triton in Rome, sculpted by Italian artist Gian Lorenzo Bernini in the mid-1600s. The fountain, considered to be one of Rome's most beautiful, features the half-man, half-fish god seated on an open shell and blowing his signature conch.

Nymphs, Sprites, and Other Minor Divinities

ots of lesser water deities also delighted the ancient world. The Greeks had a special fondness for nymphs, who had the sleek, svelte bodies of beautiful young women or girls—no scaly appendages. Sometimes the nymphs rode dolphins or other water creatures—a fishy link with their merfolk relatives. Our word nymph comes from the Greek nymphē. In English it means a young girl, often with seductive qualities. The Greeks categorized these feminine spirits according to the type of water they inhabited.

- ≈ *Oceanids* lived in the oceans.
- ≈ *Nereids* resided in the seas and the foam along rocky coastlines.
- ≈ *Naiads* preferred freshwater—lakes, rivers and streams, marshes, and even fountains.

But the Greeks weren't the only ones who believed in water deities. Early Europeans, from the Mediterranean regions to Scandinavia, believed in water sprites—some playful, some dangerous—and they told tantalizing stories about mysterious beings who could breathe both water and air. Sprite comes from the Latin *spiritus*, meaning "spirit." These elemental spirits cavorted in lakes, rivers, and waterfalls, sporting human-like bodies with blue-green skin. But these spirits lacked the mermaid's characteristic fishtail—that feature was tacked on later, after sailors spread stories of mermaids around the world.

In Africa, water spirits including Mami Wata (see Chapter 8) not only appeared with fishtails, they also showed up with the extremities of snakes or crocodiles attached to their human torsos. Some of these spirits may have spawned tales of mermaids in the Caribbean regions, when slaves brought their folklore with them to the West.

MARRIAGE LORE

Greek lore says that if a man manages to steal a water nymph's scarf he can force her to marry him.

Mixed Marriages

 ome folklore suggests that mermaids evolved from trysts between gods and water nymphs, or between sea deities and humans. Greek and Roman gods frequently crossed species lines in their amorous adventures. The lusty Olympian Zeus, for instance, impregnated an oceanid named Metis, and Apollo was besotted with Chlidanope, a beautiful freshwater nymph.

Tales of "mixed marriages" between divinities, spirits, humans, and creatures of many types abound in mythology (remember the romance between a shepherd lad and the Assyrian goddess Atargatis, who supposedly launched the mermaid race?). Mermaids themselves frequently seek human partners, as did the little mermaid in Hans Christian Andersen's famous story and the Greek ondines.

Myths, folklore, and occult texts dating back to ancient Greece speak of water elementals called ondines or undines. Elementals are nonphysical beings who inhabit the four elements—earth, air, fire, and water—and they can sometimes be seen by humans. Although modern occultism holds that ondines exist in all bodies of water, they were once believed to be freshwater spirits who lived in ponds, lakes, and waterfalls.

Ondines may have served as prototypes for mermaids. Like mermaids, they possess beautiful singing voices and are said to live forever. Some legends attest that an ondine can only gain a soul if she bears a child to a human man, an idea that reinforces the myths of unions between spirits and morals—as well as lore about mermaids' desire for human mates. But in the German tale *Sleep of Ondine*, a mermaid's marriage to a human turns into a tragedy. The heroine, a water nymph appropriately named Ondine, loses her immortality—and her mortal husband—after she bears him a child.

> "These Nature spirits were held in the highest esteem,
> and propitiatory offerings were made to them.
> Occasionally, as the result of atmospheric conditions or the
> peculiar sensitiveness of the devotee, they became visible."
>
> —Manly P. Hall, *The Secret Teachings of All Ages*

THE CURSE OF ONDINE

The "Curse of Ondine" is a term for congenital central hypoventilation syndrome, a potentially fatal form of sleep apnea. In the story *Sleep of Ondine*, the water nymph curses her husband when she catches him with another female by saying, "For as long as you are awake, you shall breathe. But should you ever fall into sleep, that breath will desert you." When he could no longer stay awake and succumbed to sleep, he died.

Wishful Delusions?

"In several European languages, including French, Italian, and Spanish, the word for 'mermaid' is actually a derivative of 'siren,' while manatees and dugongs, those sea-mammals so often presented as the reality behind mermaid sightings, belong to the order Sirenia."

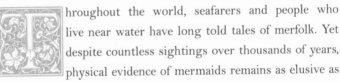

—Gail-Nina Anderson, "Mermaids in Myth and Art," *www.forteantimes.com*

hroughout the world, seafarers and people who live near water have long told tales of merfolk. Yet despite countless sightings over thousands of years, physical evidence of mermaids remains as elusive as that of Bigfoot. Some mermaid debunkers dismiss sailors' claims as the wishful delusions of men who've been too long at sea or have drunk too much rum—or both. Perhaps the mermaid's elusiveness is part of her mystique.

Other researchers suggest that the so-called "mermaids" seafarers reported seeing were really manatees, dugongs, or the now-extinct Steller's sea cows. These aquatic mammals have large eyes and rather human-like faces, and at night or from a distance they might be mistaken for the legendary mermaids.

During his voyage back from the New World in 1493, Christopher Columbus wrote of spotting three mermaids playing in the waves in the Caribbean. Quite likely he actually saw manatees, for he reported that the mermaids were "not half as beautiful as they are painted" and their faces looked more like men's than women's.

Adult manatees and dugongs, however, grow up to 12 feet in length and weigh more than 1,000 pounds, whereas mermaids are usually described as being the size of humans. Furthermore, manatees prefer warm water—coastal waters, shallow rivers, and bays—and the largest manatee population today lives in Florida's waters. This makes it unlikely that English explorer Henry Hudson saw manatees when he reported spying mermaids in the frigid sea near the Arctic Circle in 1608, during his search for a Northwest Passage.

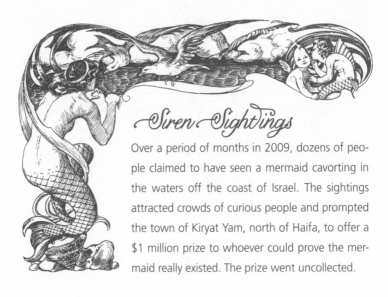

Siren Sightings

Over a period of months in 2009, dozens of people claimed to have seen a mermaid cavorting in the waters off the coast of Israel. The sightings attracted crowds of curious people and prompted the town of Kiryat Yam, north of Haifa, to offer a $1 million prize to whoever could prove the mermaid really existed. The prize went uncollected.

Aquatic Anima

oted Swiss analyst Carl G. Jung (1875–1961) proposed the idea that each person, regardless of gender, psychologically has both a masculine and a feminine side. He used the term *anima* to describe the feminine part of a man's psyche, and noted that often men repress this part of themselves. According to Jung, when someone doesn't integrate a facet of his nature he tends to project it outward and see it represented in his external circumstances—and he's usually both attracted and repelled by what he sees.

Women sometimes report seeing mermaids, but mostly it's men who spot them. And though mermen have been sighted throughout the centuries, mermaids make up the vast majority of these mysterious sea beings—at least according to legends and recorded accounts. Thus, Jungian analysts might describe mermaids as symbols of the *anima*, desirable, yet frightening, and infinitely fascinating as they emerge from the secret depths of the subconscious.

Could our current fascination with mermaids signify a resurgence of feminine power at the end of the Age of Pisces (the sign astrologers connect with the sea)? Mermaids are not only alluring; they're also agents of life and death. Just as Ariel, the little mermaid in the Disney film, rescues the shipwrecked prince, mermaids may have shown up to redeem a world mankind has brought to the brink of ruin.

We may also be connected to mermaids in a physical way as well. Science tells us that mermaids' oceanic home is also the source of human life—we all started out as aquatic creatures eons ago. As embryos, we developed from fish-like beings in the salty amniotic fluid of our mothers' wombs, in order to finally become Homo sapiens. If that's so, perhaps we share a similar ancestry with these mysterious and alluring water spirits. Maybe there's a bit of merfolk in all of us.

"Mermaids and other female water spirits have appeared in folklore and religions around the world for many centuries. They may be viewed as symbols both of men's idealization of the feminine and of men's fear of women."

—Professor Jonathan Cheek, "The Mermaid Myth"

The Sirens' Song

ermaids are notorious for enchanting male sailors with their beauty and irresistible singing voices—and then luring the bedazzled men to watery graves. In Homer's 3,000-year-old epic poem *Odyssey*, the hero, Odysseus, is lashed to the mast of his ship to prevent him from jumping overboard when he hears the Sirens' seductive voices, and his sailors stuff wax in their ears for protection.

Modern mermaids, however, have relinquished their devastating power over men. Yes, they still sing, but their songs are upbeat and pleasing instead of mesmerizingly murderous. Still sexy, but hardly siren-like, today's comely creatures are fun-loving and flirtatious rather than frightening. In TV commercials they prefer to entice men into buying beer or blue jeans rather than dragging them down into the ocean's depths.

In short, the mermaid has become a merchandising tool. Retail stores and online shops offer mermaid outfits for little girls—and grownups, too. You can buy mermaid lunchboxes, beach towels, jewelry, dishes, sheets, and Christmas tree ornaments, to name a few. Hollywood and Madison Avenue have tamed the mermaid. Her mystique has diminished, partly because she's omnipresent now instead of rare. Today's mermaid could be the girl next door (except for her fins, of course). Unlike her sultry, siren ancestors, the modern mermaid is safe—and it seems we prefer her that way.

Fanciful Fins

aybe you weren't born a mermaid, but don't let that stop you from fulfilling your fantasy. These days anybody can become a mermaid—well, at least you can look like one. The first order of business is acquiring a mermaid tail. Online stores offer plenty of options for wannabe mermaids of all ages—and in all price ranges. Some of these fishy appendages can be worn in the water, like swimsuits. Others are designed specifically to attract attention on land.

Most mermaid tails these days are made from neoprene, nylon spandex, silicone, or urethane—alas, real scales and fins don't last long out of water. And today's faux fins afford plenty of bling. Sequins, pretty beads, and gossamer glitz are *de rigueur* among fashionable mermaids. Most tails slip on like long, tight skirts and some come with separate, attachable dorsal fins that you can use to propel yourself around the pool.

Of course, color is a consideration when it comes to choosing the right tail for you. Most mermaid tails take their inspiration from the sea itself and greens, blues, and watery shades predominate. But if you prefer purple, red, or yellow tails you won't be disappointed—there's something for everyone.

Depending on your finances, you can purchase a basic mermaid tail for about $60—or you can order custom-made extremities that run in the thousands of dollars. You can even rent a fishtail if masquerading as a mermaid is only a passing fancy. For more information, visit *http://mermaidtails.net* for a listing of mermaid tails and other accouterments for sale.

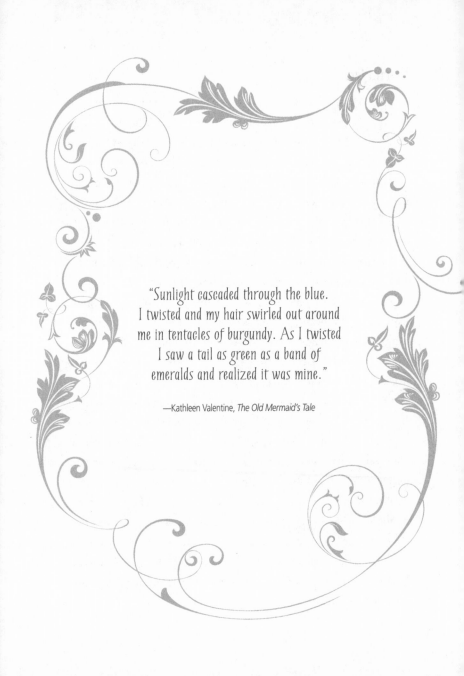

"Sunlight cascaded through the blue.
I twisted and my hair swirled out around
me in tentacles of burgundy. As I twisted
I saw a tail as green as a band of
emeralds and realized it was mine."

—Kathleen Valentine, *The Old Mermaid's Tale*

CHAPTER 2

WHAT DO
Mermaids Look Like?

WHEN YOU PICTURE A MERMAID, what do you see? A mythical creature whose head and body, from the pelvis up, resemble that of a gorgeous human female? A creature with long, flowing hair, smooth skin, and full, shapely breasts? A beauty who, from the pelvis down, sports the greenish, scaly tail of a fish? This general description covers the most basic characteristics we've come to associate with mermaids over the centuries—but various cultures in different times and places have put their own spins on these seagoing, hybrid beauties. Some mermaids are innocently beautiful, others are terrifyingly seductive. What does the true mermaid look like? Let's find out.

Fish Tales

"That sea-maid's form, of pearly light,
Was whiter than the downy spray,
And round her bosom, heaving bright,
Her glossy, yellow ringlets play."

—from John Leyden's nineteenth-century ballad, "The Mermaid"

lthough we're used to thinking of mermaids as beautiful, myth and folklore tell us that this wasn't always the case. The *Speculum Regale*, a thirteenth-century Norwegian text (also called the *King's Mirror*), described mermaids as Neanderthal-like beasts with fish-tails and scales on their lower bodies, large webbed hands, terrifying faces, wide mouths, and wrinkled cheeks—hardly the comely creatures we think of today!

The ancient Babylonian god Ea (or Oannes) initially appeared on the scene wearing a cloak made of fish scales; later images show him as a half-man, half-fish merman. Pliny the Elder, who lived in Italy during the first century C.E., wrote some of the earliest "scientific" accounts of mermaids in his extensive compilation *Natural History*—he described them as "rough and scaled all over."

The Assyrian goddess Atargatis, who legend says became our first mermaid, is depicted on ancient coins as a fish standing upright on its tail and wearing the head of a human woman. Some early artwork shows her with two legs as well as a tail.

The Roman poet Ovid described the Greek merman, Triton, as having the upper body of a human and the tail of a fish, but his shoulders were "barnacled with sea-shells." The infamous Greek Sirens, whose enchanting songs lured seamen to their deaths, started off as bird-women, and only later exchanged their feathers for fishtails. Other sources report merfolk as lacking scales and tails altogether.

Siren Sightings

In July 1833, six fishermen off Scotland's Isle of Yell hauled aboard a mermaid who had become tangled in their lines. The men described her as being about three feet in length with "bristles extending from her head to her shoulders that could be raised or lowered." Other notations concerning the incident added that the mermaid lacked scales, fins, or gills. The skipper told the story to a Mr. Edmondson who repeated it to a Natural History Professor at the University of Edinburgh. When all was said and done it had been decided that it was "quite impossible" for six Shetland fishermen to mistake another type of sea-creature for a mermaid.

Tailless Water Maidens

he numerous water nymphs who populated ancient Greek mythology had the lush, two-legged bodies of young human females, rather than the fishy lower parts of the mermaids we know today—which were perhaps inspired by these nymphs. Without the encumbrance of a fish's tail, these nubile nymphs could freely cavort with males, both human and divine—a pastime their scaly successors were anatomically forced to forego. These nymphs' "fish" ties instead were expressed via association, such as their penchant for riding on dolphins.

The same fishy connection shows up in early images and descriptions of Aphrodite, the Greek goddess of love from whom some sources suggest mermaids evolved. Often this beautiful, woman-like deity is depicted with her companion, a sacred dolphin. However, her male escorts, the Tritons, featured fishtails below their waists. Aphrodite's Roman counterpart, Venus, always appears as a lovely, human-shaped goddess. In Botticelli's famous fifteenth-century painting *Birth of Venus* (now in the Uffizi Gallery in Florence, Italy) she emerges from the sea as a nude, smooth-skinned, adult female, borne on the waves in an open scallop shell, suggesting another type of link between human and sea creature.

The water spirits known as ondines also lacked scales, fins, or other fishy attributes—though like the water nymphs, they sometimes traveled on the backs of dolphins or large fish. In *A Midsummer Night's Dream*, Shakespeare's character Oberon speaks of seeing a mermaid riding on the back of a dolphin. Shakespearean scholars propose that the Bard might have been referring to Mary Queen of Scots, who married the Dauphin (dolphin) of France.

IN SEARCH OF ONDINES

In his 1928 tome *The Secret Teachings of All Ages*, Manly P. Hall wrote that according to ancient sources, "In general, nearly all the undines [ondines] closely resembled human beings in appearance and size, though the ones inhabiting small streams and fountains were of correspondingly lesser proportions. It was believed that these water spirits were occasionally capable of assuming the appearance of normal human beings and actually associating with men and women."

Mermaids in Art

 ver since artists first painted on papyrus scrolls, they've chosen mermaids as subjects. From the frozen Arctic regions to the salubrious South Sea Islands, people have depicted their conceptions of mermaids in wood, stone, bone, cloth, and metal. In some cases, creating an image of a mermaid served talismanic purposes. Sailors carved wooden figureheads of mermaids and attached them to the prows of their ships to provide protection during sea voyages. Those who practice Vodou fashion shimmering mermaid banners from sequins to attract prosperity and love. In some cultures, people sought the magic of mermaids to help them catch fish, bring rain, or heal the sick.

Mermaids from different parts of the world bear many similarities —fishy attributes, long flowing hair, and the upper bodies of beautiful young women. But there are differences, too. In Africa, India, and Australia, mermaids sometimes sport the tails of snakes, lizards, or even crocodiles instead of fish. Some early mermaids had two tails, or a split tail that resolved the question of how can mermaids have sex.

Of course, the mermaid's sultry sexuality is her most enticing quality—and it's the rare mermaid who doesn't tempt and tantalize. Most likely, this seductiveness evolved from the early fertility and creator goddesses, who not accidentally ruled over the waters of the world. And it's this seductiveness that caused the mermaid's popularity as a subject for artwork to burgeon during the Victorian period, despite the puritanical attitudes of the time. Mermaids gave artists a sexy subject to paint when social norms repressed sex— and gentlemen collectors liked looking at naked ladies hanging on their walls. In fact, many of our present-day ideas about what mermaids look like come from the paintings of that era.

MYSTERIOUS MERMAIDS

In 1899, noted Austrian artist Gustav Klimt painted mermaids—but his water spirits bear no resemblance to the half-woman, half-fish beauties with which we're familiar. Instead they look like women's faces peering out from dark body bags and convey the sinister side of these mysterious beings.

Artists' Influence

"Beauty seems to be the keynote of the water spirits.
Wherever we find them pictured in art or sculpture,
they abound in symmetry and grace."

—Manly P. Hall, The Secret Teachings of All Ages

uring the Victorian period, mermaids captured the imagination of painters who portrayed them as lush, lovely creatures who captivated art collectors just as they had captivated seafarers for centuries. The paintings of Victorian-era artists such as John William Waterhouse and Frederic Leighton helped to form our ideas of what mermaids look like. These lush, romantic pictures blend tantalizing sensuality with the prudishness of the time period; at a time when human women concealed their charms beneath layers of clothing, mermaids openly displayed theirs with tantalizing abandon. But no matter how enticing a mermaid may be, her tail—the ultimate chastity belt— prevented her from engaging in sexual relations with human men.

Not all artists saw fit to portray mermaids with the familiar fish-below-the-waist bodies. In 1896, Edvard Munch (best known for his haunting picture *The Scream*) painted his *Mermaid* with a mostly human form—her fishy tail starts at her knees. John William Waterhouse's sultry *The Siren* wears scales only from her calves down. In René Magritte's *The Forbidden Universe*, the mermaid's tail extends a bit further up her legs, but only to mid-thigh, leaving her pertinent parts exposed and accessible. These depictions slyly sidestep the idea of enforced chasteness and hint at the

John William Waterhouse's *A Mermaid*

possibility of coupling with human males. Magritte's earlier picture, *Collective Invention*, turns the tables on the mermaid myth—it features a hybrid creature with the upper body of a fish and the lower body of a woman!

Early representations of the African Mami Wata (see Chapter 8) show the familiar mermaid form. But all that changed after German artist Felix Schlesinger's Art Nouveau chromolithograph, *Der Schlagenbandinger* appeared. It depicted a sensual, black-haired, dark-skinned snake charmer with an anaconda wrapped around her shapely, woman's body—and so Mami Wata continues to be envisioned today.

SIREN SLANG

During the 1700s and 1800s, the terms "mermaid" and "siren" served as code words for prostitutes.

Seaside Shapeshifting

 he folklore of many cultures portrays merfolk as shapeshifters who can magically transform themselves from fish-tailed hybrids into two-legged humans. Some of these beings are said to live among people for extended periods of time, forming families and raising children with human mates—who may or may not realize their true natures.

The selkies can change into seals.

The legends of Ireland, Scotland, Wales, and the Shetland and Faroe islands speak of selkies or seal people who don the skins of seals in order to glide through the ocean. When they decide to come ashore—usually to take human lovers—selkies remove their sealskins and walk on land as ordinary women. Should a man discover and take possession of a selkie's pelt, he can prevent her from returning to the sea.

A SELKIE SECRET

The 1994 movie *The Secret of Roan Inish*, directed by John Sayles, tells the story of a selkie trapped by a fisherman who steals her sealskin to keep her on land with him. The mixed couple bears children together, but she longs for the sea. When she finds the sealskin her husband hid from her, she realizes she's been tricked and returns to her home in the ocean.

The nixes can transform themselves into humans,
animals, fish, or reptiles.

According to Teutonic legends, the nixes (or nixies) could change shape at will, taking on the forms of humans, fish, or snakes. Jacob Grimm—one-half of the Brothers Grimm of fairy-tale fame—believed these water spirits to be higher beings who sometimes assumed the bodies of animals or people. When in human form, Grimm said a nixie could be recognized by a small slit in the ear or the wet hem of her skirt.

The yawkyawks can shapeshift into dragonflies.

The yawkyawks, said to inhabit the sacred waterholes of Australia, usually fit the conventional image of mermaids, except their long, green hair looks like seaweed. At night, however, these shapeshifters walk the land on human legs or assume the shape of dragonflies if they want to flit about.

It seems these fluid females aren't locked into a specific form or locale—they can look or move about as they please. Their changeable nature simply adds intrigue and appeal.

A MOVIE MERMAID

The 1984 comedy *Splash*, starring Daryl Hannah, gives the mermaid's shapeshifting nature a new twist. In the movie, when her fishtail dries, it transforms into a woman's legs.

Undersea Curiosity

 any mermaids seem as intrigued with humans as we are with them—that's why they venture onto land to interact with people. Irish tales speak of the merrows, or moruachs, whose curiosity about the human world leads them to take on completely human forms so they can mingle with people undetected. Residents of the Orkney Islands, off Scotland's northeast tip, warn of dangerous shapeshifters known as finfolk. These creatures disguise themselves as beautiful women or fishermen in order to come on land and capture unwitting victims, whom they take to their underwater lands as slaves. Old Norse and Germanic myths describe a male water spirit known as a Fosse-Grim, a virtuoso violinist whose music attracts human women to him. Supposedly, he can transform himself into animals, fish, or floating objects if he wishes.

In mermaid myths, transformation is a key theme. Does the shift from water spirit to human, described in so many stories, symbolize our own evolution from creatures of the sea to human beings—and our own longing to return to the source from which we came? You see, although mermaids straddle the worlds of nature and civilization, they frequently seem ill at ease when living among humans. They may come ashore to mate with mortal men, but after a time they pine for their watery homes and eventually return to the sea. The reverse situation occurs in Matthew Arnold's Victorian poem "The Forsaken Merman." In it a human mother leaves her merman husband and their children in the sea and goes back to live again on land. Like humans, mermaids want to see and experience different places. But in the end, they, too, get homesick, and it's the rare mermaid who leaves the sea forever.

 ## HOW TO ATTRACT A MERMAID

Want to attract a mermaid? Give her something shiny. Mermaids especially like red, orange, and yellow baubles that remind them of the sun.

MAIDEN OR MERMAID?

Marina, the heroine of Hans Christian Andersen's *The Little Mermaid* (renamed Ariel in Disney's movie version of the Danish fairy tale) falls in love with a human prince and longs to leave her underwater home for life on land. However, Marina/Ariel can only become human if she sacrifices her beautiful singing voice. Edvard Eriksen's statue *The Little Mermaid* in Copenhagen, Andersen's birthplace, depicts her partly with legs and also the remnants of a tail, perhaps to remind tourists of her hybrid origins.

CAN YOU TALK TO MERMAIDS?

Want to converse with a mermaid? First you'll have to learn her language—and that might not be so easy (it's not on Rosetta Stone). According to Bard Judith in "The Merfolk," mermaids speak a language called Mermish that is "simplistic, heavily aspirated, and used only above water . . . a combination of two languages, mostly coastal human dialects mixed with Mersong. Below the water they communicate in a series of whistles, fluting sounds, sub- and super-sonic pulses which humans cannot hear"—though fish, whales, and dolphins may understand merfolk.

Twin-Tailed Mermaids

ack in 1971, when Starbucks started selling coffee beans in Seattle, Washington, the company's logo featured a mermaid that deviated from the image most of us hold. Rather than the familiar single fishtail comprising the lower half of her body, this aquatic beauty sported twin tails, which she held up in her hands on either side of her woman's bare-breasted torso.

Over time, Starbucks modified the mermaid to make her less naughty. In 1987, logo designers covered up her breasts with her long, wavy hair. When Starbucks became a publicly traded company in 1992, the logo underwent yet another change, this time obscuring the mermaid's lower body so that only a hint of her split-tail remained in the stylized, sanitized version. To commemorate its fortieth anniversary, Starbucks refined the logo once again in 2011, eliminating the familiar lifesaver-like circle around the mermaid along with the company's name.

The twin-tailed or split-tailed mermaid isn't something the Starbucks marketing team dreamt up to entice customers, although she conveys obvious sexual connotations. She dates back to ancient times, turning up in the art and mythology of various countries, and recalls the old matriarchal belief systems that predated the dominant patriarchal religions of today. This sexy siren is a cross between the early Celtic fertility goddess Sheila-na-gig, who squats and suggestively shows off her feminine secrets, and the more typical mermaid. She blatantly separates her tail into two parts in order to reveal her genitalia—and presumably make sex with human men possible.

"[They] prominently display their genitalia to signify the power of female sexuality and fertility. These images are also quite prominent in the decoration of sacred sites in general and are thought to be a legacy of the older Goddess religions whose holy sites were usually taken over by later religions. The shape of the genitalia in these squatting figures is also symbolic of the vesica piscis, the 'vessel of the fish' . . . "

—Heinz Insu Fenkl, "The Mermaid"

Spiritual Sirens

he image of the split-tailed mermaid appears as a decorative motif, rendered in stone, wood, and mosaic, on many early churches and cathedrals in Europe. She graces the French churches Notre Dame de Cunault, the Basilique St. Julien de Brioude, St. Pierre de la Bouisse, and St. Pierre Bessuéjouls. She also turns up in Italian churches, including San Pietro in Ciel d'Oro, Pavia, Santa Croce in Parma, and Cattedrale di Santa Maria Annunciata in Puglia. England, too, has its twin-tailed mermaids, unabashedly displaying their charms in the Church of St. George in Hertfordshire and Lancashire's Cartmel Priory Church, where she also holds the typical mermaid's mirror and comb.

Mermaids of the usual variety also appear in plenty of churches in Europe and the British Isles. In times when most of the populace was illiterate, pictures conveyed themes and morals to the pious. Christianity connects fish with Jesus, the "fisher of men," and Christians in general. Mermaids symbolized the sins of vanity and lust. When churchgoers saw mermaids swimming with schools of fish on the walls of their chapels, they recognized it as a message to avoid temptation that would lead them to fall into the mermaid's clutches.

Of course, the church fathers played up stories of the mermaid's penchant for drowning men who succumbed to her wiles. Nevertheless, these sexy sirens serve as artful adornments that may have distracted or delighted many a bored parishioner over the centuries.

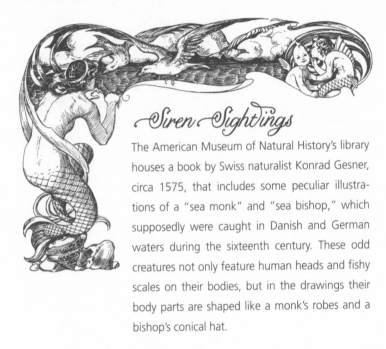

Siren Sightings

The American Museum of Natural History's library houses a book by Swiss naturalist Konrad Gesner, circa 1575, that includes some peculiar illustrations of a "sea monk" and "sea bishop," which supposedly were caught in Danish and German waters during the sixteenth century. These odd creatures not only feature human heads and fishy scales on their bodies, but in the drawings their body parts are shaped like a monk's robes and a bishop's conical hat.

Reptilian Water Deities

egends of deities with snake, lizard, or crocodile body parts emerge from many cultures. These scaly hybrids are said to rule the waters of the world—and like mermaids and other water spirits, they possess mystical and magical powers. Although Christian mythology links serpents with evil, that's not the case in other belief systems. In fact, snake gods and goddesses—as well as half-snake half-human spirits—have long been connected with creativity, wisdom, and healing.

Africans see snake gods and goddesses as creators.

Mami Wata, powerful mermaid-like water deities in many African pantheons, sometimes appear with snaky hindquarters. The African Rainbow Serpent—also spoken of in Australian mythology as a creator spirit named Ngalyod—supposedly created the world's rivers and lakes. People in parts of West Africa worship half-human, half-snake water gods with red eyes and green bodies called Nommo.

Asian myths speak of snake deities with human heads.

The ancient Chinese deities Pangu, Nuwa, Fuxi, and Gonggong had human heads and the bodies of snakes—the female goddess Nuwa supposedly created human beings. Hindu and Buddhist myths speak of divinities called nagas and naginis, human-headed snakes who lived in underwater kingdoms. They could appear as humans, serpents, or a combination of both. The great Hindu god Shiva is often depicted with two cobras coiled on his head and shoulders to protect him from harm.

Snake deities figured prominently in Aztec myths.

The powerful god Quetzalcoatl was also known as the "Feathered Serpent." The goddess Coatlicue, whom the Aztecs associated with both creativity and destruction, is often pictured as a woman wearing a skirt made of snakes.

In many of the world's myths, snakes symbolize wisdom and creative power. Mermaids with reptilian appendages instead of the usual fishtails are more than beautiful seductresses—they're goddesses.

HUMAN-SERPENT HYBRIDS

Human-serpent spirits might have influenced our conceptions of mermaids. Like merfolk, these reptilian deities can magically transform themselves from water creatures into human beings. They also display both benevolent and malevolent sides to their natures. However, these spirits generally lack one of the mermaid's most distinctive features: her mesmerizing singing voice.

Mermen

"When the *Oldenborg* sailed from Denmark to the West Indies in 1672, the crew reported seeing a Havman off the Cape of Good Hope. The ship's doctor, J. P. Cortemund, drew a picture of the being, now in the Royal Danish Library."

—Carol Rose, *Giants, Monsters, and Dragons: An Encyclopedia of Folklore, Legend, and Myth*

 ermaids fascinate people everywhere, but we don't think much about their male counterparts: mermen. Granted, the males of the species are not as common as the females, either in mythology or in reports of sightings. Nor are they as captivating. Many accounts even describe mermen as ugly and totally unappealing.

In addition to the usual fishtails, Greek legends give mermen green hair and beards—one well-known merman named Glaucus supposedly had a blue-green body as well. Irish mythology pictures mermen with long, pointed green teeth, green hair, and red pig-like snouts.

The Tritons—Aphrodite's entourage and personal bodyguards—were fishtailed male sea spirits whom mythology tells us evolved from Triton (the son of the Greek sea god Poseidon). Their ranks also contained females, called Tritonesses. According to the *Dictionary of Greek and Roman Biography and Mythology*, the males "have green hair on their head, very fine and hard scales, breathing organs below their ears, a human nose, a broad mouth, with the teeth of animals, sea-green eyes, hands rough like the surface of a shell, and instead of feet, a tail like that of dolphins."

Exceptions to these unpleasant mermen exist, of course. The Havman of Scandinavian legend, for instance, is usually described as quite handsome. The Germanic nix—perhaps related to the charismatic character Fosse-Grim—seems to exude attractive qualities, too, for legends say human women regularly fell in love with him.

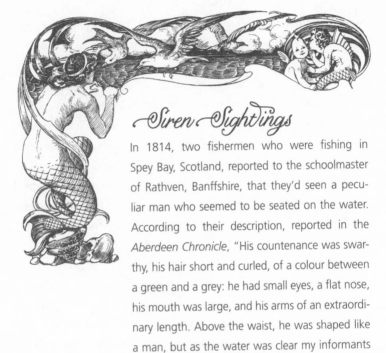

Siren Sightings

In 1814, two fishermen who were fishing in Spey Bay, Scotland, reported to the schoolmaster of Rathven, Banffshire, that they'd seen a peculiar man who seemed to be seated on the water. According to their description, reported in the *Aberdeen Chronicle*, "His countenance was swarthy, his hair short and curled, of a colour between a green and a grey: he had small eyes, a flat nose, his mouth was large, and his arms of an extraordinary length. Above the waist, he was shaped like a man, but as the water was clear my informants could perceive that from the waist downwards, his body tapered considerably or, as they expressed it, like a large fish without scales but could not see the extremity."

A Mermaid's Countenance

ur conceptions of merfolk have changed over time, gradually evolving into the lovely creatures we know today. Some mermaid historians explain that once sailors began traveling the seven seas—and swapping mermaid stories—a generally accepted picture of these enigmatic creatures developed.

According to *The Standard Dictionary of Folklore, Mythology, and Legend*, typical mermaids exhibit the following traits:

- ≈ Bodies tend to be graceful, slim, and about the size of small humans: males are approximately 5 feet 6 inches in length and weigh about 110 to 130 pounds; females are a few inches shorter, weighing 95 to 115 pounds.
- ≈ Skin color can be pale or brilliantly colored: black, green, blue, white, yellow, turquoise, or red, and may be mottled like that of fish.
- ≈ Hair is usually long, often streaked with lighter shades than the principal color, and is sometimes braided or beaded (other sources say hair color can be anything from blonde to black, even green, blue, or purple).
- ≈ Hands are webbed, and fingers may lack fingernails; other sources describe the nails as looking like shells.
- ≈ Eyes, though similar in appearance to humans', are large and have both eyelids and an additional, protective inner shield; the eyes are usually black, blue, or green.

- ≈ Two "separate but complementary pulmonary and cardio circuits . . . allow them to breathe in water or on land." They have gills below their ears, which close when they are on land.
- ≈ They rarely wear clothing, but may don bracelets, necklaces, earrings, torques, armbands, belts, and anklets.

 ## DISSECTING MERMAIDS

Some researchers, such as the mysterious mermaid enthusiast known only as the Water Mage Ge Wonderwed of Carmalad, claim to have examined the anatomy of mermaids in great depth and detail. In the essay "Mermaids: A Myth Being Dissected," the Water Mage reports that these enigmatic creatures have the following characteristics:

- ◆ Their bodily fluids are turquoise.
- ◆ Oil-secreting glands along the hairline offer protection during immersion in water—perhaps the reason mermaids are often seen combing their hair.
- ◆ They have lips, tongues, and rows of small, pointed teeth.
- ◆ A strong, bony "girdle" at the waist, connected to the backbone, supports the muscular tail.
- ◆ They have a single lung and small hearts, but lack the other internal organs of humans.
- ◆ Reproductive organs and capabilities are uncertain.

"Every little girl's dream is to be a
mermaid or to see a mermaid . . .
People from different cultures and
centuries have the same idea of what
mermaids are . . . that's maybe a cool
thing to think about."

—Emma Roberts

Wonders of the Deep

*"I must be a mermaid . . . I have no fear of depths
and a great fear of shallow living."*

 —Writer Anaïs Nin

o what, exactly, are mermaids? We may never be able to answer that question—and maybe we don't really want to. Mermaids' mystique—like that of Bigfoot, ETs, and the Loch Ness monster—is part of their appeal. Whether merfolk live among us on Earth, shapeshift so they can visit us from other realms, serve as symbols of our collective unconscious, or are purely products of our imagination remains a mystery.

One thing seems certain: mermaids are *not* Homo sapiens, nor fish, nor are they a blend of the two. Mermaids are a species unto themselves, totally unique and miraculous. They're a type of sea mammal, certainly, for like all mammals, they have hair and are able to nurse their young. But perhaps mermaids represent a wondrous part of ourselves, a part we can only discover if we plunge deep down inside. . . .

Siren Sightings

After a stormy night in 1870, a mermaid was spotted playing in the water near a beach in Benbecula, Outer Hebrides. When the townspeople realized what she was, they tried to capture her in a net, but their efforts were in vain; the mermaid quickly swam out of harm's way. She had almost escaped when the town bully hit her in the head with a rock. Her body washed up on the beach the next day. According to Tom Williams of the *Naples Daily News*, "Upon close inspection, everyone agreed this was a true mermaid. She had the body of a child with well-developed breasts but below the waist she had scales and a tail like a fish." She appeared so human that the town's officials ordered her body to be buried in the town cemetery.

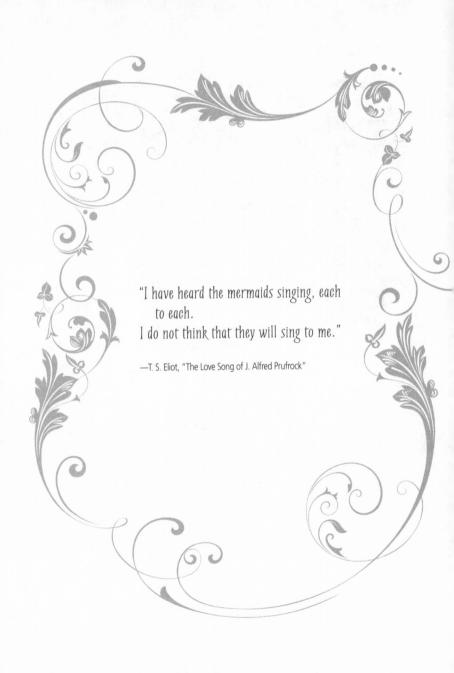

"I have heard the mermaids singing, each
to each.
I do not think that they will sing to me."

—T. S. Eliot, "The Love Song of J. Alfred Prufrock"

CHAPTER 3

Mermaids' Attributes, Behavior, AND Environs

IN ADDITION TO THEIR FISHY TAILS and human torsos, the traits and behaviors of mermaids are similar in the various mythologies of the world. These attributes became more homogenized during the middle of the second millennium C.E., as trade routes expanded and seamen journeyed far and wide, sharing their "fish stories" with peoples of various lands. Later, immigrants and slaves brought their mermaid legends with them when they relocated, and those tales merged with the folklore that already existed in their new homes.

However, certain common mermaid characteristics figured prominently in the mythology of diverse cultures, long before the periods of travel and exploration in the late Middle Ages and the Renaissance. Chief among these are mermaids' enchanting voices, their sensuality, and their destructive potential—all of which lie at the core of the mermaid mystique.

The Mermaid's Song

"[T]he secret of the power in their song: it is the sound of the subversive, luring us from the orderly conscious world down to the depth of the world of dreams, and the harder we try to ignore that singing, the more we desperately want to hear it."

—Meri Lao, *Seduction and the Secret Power of Women: The Lure of Sirens and Mermaids*

 ccording to nearly all legends and stories, a mermaid's voice isn't merely melodious enough to rival the greatest of operatic divas. It's so mesmerizing that men who hear it go wild with delight and jump from their boats or rush into the sea—and subsequently drown. Some sailors, captivated and disoriented by the mermaids' hauntingly beautiful singing, run their ships aground on rocky shores and, in a state of delicious delirium, they go to their watery graves.

Interestingly, among the numerous reports given throughout the ages by people who claim to have seen mermaids, few mention hearing the infamous singing. Perhaps if they had heard the mermaids' songs, they might not have lived to tell the tales!

"In stories, poems and myths, hearing a mermaid's song was considered a haunting and hazardous experience. Typically, it lured the listener to toss aside safety and sometimes his or her whole, known world, and plunge into the waves. Such a leap could bring doom or it could bring salvation. Sometimes it brought both. The mermaid's song inevitably calls us to the unknown, to the impassioned world of change and possibility. Ultimately mermaids persist in the imagination because they represent a primal human need: to dive deep into the mystery of our un-lived life."

—Sue Monk Kidd, bestselling author of *The Mermaid Chair* and *The Secret Life of Bees*

MAPPING MERMAIDS

As early sailors ventured farther out to sea, mapmakers began picturing mermaids and other marine oddities on maps. Mermaids may have been intended as symbols of the sea itself, or as alerts to seafarers of the mysteries they might encounter on their voyages. Mermaids frequently appear on medieval *mappa mundi*, such as the thirteenth-century rendering signed by Richard de Haldingham e de Lafford and now housed in Britain's Hereford Cathedral.

Literary Accounts of Mermaids' Songs

he ancient *One Thousand and One Nights* says that mermaids' songs rendered sailors helpless and lured them to their doom. The infamous Sirens of ancient Greek myth are presented as melodious but malevolent temptresses—no man could resist their tantalizing singing. In the 3,000-year-old *Odyssey*, Odysseus (or Ulysses in Latin) is warned about the Sirens' powers; he therefore ties himself to his ship's mast and his sailors put wax in their ears so they won't be driven mad by the enchantresses' songs. Our modern-day word "siren," rooted in the Greek myths of the Sirens of old, has the connotation of a seductive and potentially dangerous human femme fatale.

Folklore remains pretty quiet on the subject of mermen's singing ability. Some sources report the males as having "silvery" or "fluted" voices, though nothing as exquisite as those of the females. One Cornish legend tells of a handsome young man from the town of Zennor who goes to live with the mermaids—yet people in the town still say they hear his beautiful tenor voice wafting on the waves. But just because mermen don't possess the bewitchingly beautiful voices of the females of the species doesn't mean that they lack musical talent. The Scandinavian Havman is said to be an accomplished violinist who enchants women with his skillful playing, and the Greek's Triton blew a conch shell like a trumpet.

HERBERT JAMES DRAPER, *ULYSSES AND THE SIRENS*

Deadly Beauties

"[B]ehind this seductive image of the Siren lurks the a metaphor of death, for enticed by her promise and allure, generations have been lured to their certain doom in a thousand different stories that form the basis of powerful and enduring myths and legends that continue today."

 —Beatrice Phillpotts, *Mermaids*

o mermaids intend to sing mariners into "the big sleep"? Or do their victims simply overreact when they hear the otherworldly beauty of the music? It's a subject for debate. It's been speculated that sailors, upon observing mermaids floating in the waves, think they see drowning women and jump overboard to rescue them—but in the process the well-meaning seamen drown instead.

Some stories say that mermaids drag men they fancy down into the depths and accidentally drown them, not realizing that humans can't breathe underwater. Other tales say humans who've been drawn into the mermaids' underwater realms remain there, transformed into merfolk themselves.

Hans Christian Andersen's popular fairy tale "The Little Mermaid" offers yet another perspective. In it the author explains that the mermaid's song is a compassionate attempt to calm the fears of sailors who are about to drown in a storm at sea. "They had more beautiful voices than any human being could have; and before the approach of a storm, and when they expected a ship would be lost, they swam before the vessel, and sang sweetly of the delights to be found in the depths of the sea, and begging the sailors not to fear if they sank to the bottom."

"A mermaid found a swimming lad,

Picked him for her own,

Pressed her body to his body,

Laughed; and plunging down

Forgot in cruel happiness

That even lovers drown."

—William Butler Yeats, "A Man Young and Old"

MILITARY MERFOLK

Mermaids may be dangerous, but they don't normally attack people—they use their feminine wiles to lure men to their deaths. Mermen, however, can be more warlike. They're said to fashion weapons from the body parts of other sea creatures—coral, shells, bones, and the teeth of large aquatic predators.

The Tempest

 any legends link mermaids with storms and even blame them for whipping up tempests at sea in order to sink ships. Some old English stories portrayed mermaids as evil omens and portents of bad luck. It's said that if a sailor spotted a mermaid, it meant bad weather was coming and he'd never return home again.

Another belief, explained in the twelfth-century text known as the *Speculum Regale* or *The King's Mirror*, states that when seafarers saw a mermaid at the onset of a storm, she served as an oracle and her actions let them know if they'd survive or perish. According to this theory, the mermaid dives underwater and brings up a fish. If she plays with the fish or throws it at the boat, death is imminent. If she eats the fish or tosses it back into the water, away from the ship, the sailors will make it through the tempest alive.

Ominous depictions of mermaids were encouraged by the Catholic Church during the Middle Ages. Medieval church fathers linked mermaids with the deadly sins of vanity and lust, as well as the alluring powers of women in general. Some churches displayed images of mermaids swimming with fish or starfish (which symbolized Christians) as warnings against sexual temptations. If a mermaid held a fish in her hands, it signified that a Christian had succumbed to the sin of lust.

"Thou rememberest
Since once I sat upon a promontory,
And heard a mermaid on a Dolphin's back
Uttering such dulcet and harmonious breath,
That the rude sea grew civil at her song;
And certain stars shot madly from their spheres,
To hear the sea-maid's music."

—William Shakespeare, *A Midsummer Night's Dream*

"Slow sail'd the weary mariners and saw,
Betwixt the green brink and the running
    foam,
Sweet faces, rounded arms, and bosoms prest
To little harps of gold; and while they mused
Whispering to each other half in fear,
Shrill music reach'd them on the middle sea."

—Lord Alfred Tennyson, "The Sea-Fairies"

Bearers of Good Fortune

 ot all legends portray mermaids as dangerous. The African water deities known as Mami Wata, who often appear as mermaids, are said to heal the sick and bring good fortune. In Caribbean tradition, the water spirit/mermaid Lasirèn guides people (usually women) underwater where she confers special powers on them. Some European folklore acknowledges their potential dangers, but reminds us that mermaids, like the sea itself, can bring good things to humanity as well as bad.

Mermaids, it seems, are as changeable as the sea—serene one moment and tumultuous the next. The *Physiologus* or Bestiary (originally written in Greek, probably in the third or fourth century C.E.), was one of the most popular books during the Middle

Ages. It characterized a mermaid as "a beast of the sea wonderfully shapen as a maid from the navel upward and a fish from the navel downward, and this beast is glad and merry in tempest, and sad and heavy in fair weather."

Psychologically, mermaids have been said to represent the complexity of women's emotions, ranging from playful to stormy, as well as the light and dark sides of the human psyche. Like the fairy, whom movies and children's stories have also trivialized, mermaids can be both alluring and dangerous—certainly not something to trifle with!

MERMAID FIGUREHEADS

Throughout the centuries, sailors affixed figureheads of mermaids to the bows of their ships to ensure safe and prosperous voyages. Between about 1790 and 1825, the golden era of the clipper ships, beautifully crafted figureheads adorned British and American merchant vessels and warships alike.

Luxurious Locks

 ou'll never see a picture of a mermaid with a pixie or brush cut. One of her defining attributes is her long, flowing hair. Seafarers often report seeing a mermaid's sinuous tresses floating on the waves or twining around her body like seaweed. In some cases, artists (such as those who "cleaned up" the Starbucks logo) depict her modestly covering her breasts with her luxurious locks—something unabashed mermaids wouldn't even think of doing.

As far as the color of merfolk hair is concerned, green seems to be popular. The ancient Greek Tritons supposedly sported green hair, and legends of merfolk from Ireland and the British Isles also mention their green hair. And tales from Down Under say that the local water spirits known as yawkyawks have long hair that looks like seaweed or green algae.

In Scandinavia, however, where human blondes predominate, so do stories of golden-haired mermaids. Other folktales and sightings report that mermaids' hair can vary from palest blonde to black—and everything in between, especially the colors that remind us of the sea: green, blue, turquoise, purple, white, and silver.

Siren Sightings

In 1614, American explorer John Smith (best known for his association with Pocahontas) stated he'd seen a mermaid off the coast of Massachusetts. He described her as having long green hair and said she was "by no means unattractive."

Combs and Mirrors

If you believe what you read in mermaid myths, these lovely ladies devote a lot of time to personal grooming —specifically, combing their hair. Although they may appear devoid of other possessions—even clothing—mermaids throughout the world carry their combs and mirrors with them when they set out to entice human seafarers into their watery worlds. Countless stories speak of mermaids sitting on rocks near the ocean with their glistening tails curled about them, while they comb their long, flowing tresses and examine themselves in hand-held mirrors.

Mythology and art present numerous links between mermaids and Venus/Aphrodite, the Roman/Greek (respectively) goddess of love and beauty. Botticelli's famous painting *The Birth of Venus* depicts the goddess with abundant auburn hair, long enough to discreetly conceal her "lady parts." So perhaps it's no surprise that we see mermaids gazing into their mirrors and combing their lustrous, flowing locks—just as human women are known to do.

If you're familiar with astrology or astronomy you may notice the similarity between the mermaid's hand-held mirror and the glyph for the planet Venus (named for the Roman goddess). It's probably no accident. Take a look at that symbol—it's a circle above a plus sign—which suggests that mermaids descended from this ancient goddess of beauty and love.

THE SIN OF INDULGENCE

During the Middle Ages, the comb and mirror—two of the mermaid's most prized possessions—represented pride and vanity. British medieval churches used these symbols to caution parishioners against indulging in these sins.

Seductive Attributes

*"Hair, because of its ability to re-grow, relates to re-birth . . .
Hair that was put up or covered with a cap could, metaphorically,
be seen as lost—along with any power it was believed to possess.
Hair, then, is associated with vital female forces."*

—Patricia Radford, "Lusty Ladies: Mermaids in the Medieval Irish Church"

 woman's hair has long been counted among her most seductive attributes. Her hair was considered so enticing, in fact, that until the latter part of the twentieth century Catholic women covered their hair when they attended Mass, lest they distract men with their feminine charms. Until recently, Catholic nuns shaved their hair and veiled their heads. Buddhist nuns, too, shave their heads. Traditionally, Orthodox Jewish women wore wigs or otherwise concealed their natural hair in public. In Islamic culture today, women shroud their heads to signify modesty. So do women in Amish, Mennonite, and other conservative communities.

Obviously, there's more to a mermaid's hair than meets the eye. Barbara Walker, author of *The Woman's Dictionary of Symbols and Sacred Objects*, proposes that when a mermaid combs her hair she's performing a type of magic. Because hair traditionally represents strength, the mermaid's act of attending to her long, lustrous hair signifies her efforts to nurture and enhance her personal power.

The image of the mermaid combing her hair can also be linked to a purification ritual practiced in the Irish church, explains Patricia Radford in "Lusty Ladies: Mermaids in the Medieval Irish Church." Priests groomed their own hair with special liturgical combs in a rite intended to cleanse both body and soul. Thus, the mermaid's behavior could symbolize not only physical indulgence but transcendence as well.

WHAT'S SEXY ABOUT THE MERMAID'S COMB?

For anyone who knows Greek, a mermaid's comb is more than an implement with which to groom her long, luscious hair—it has underlying sexual implications as well. In the Greek language, the words for comb—*kteis* and *pectin*—also mean "vulva."

A Mermaid's Abode?

ccording to the accounts of sailors and people who live by the sea, mermaids frolic on the waves far out in the ocean, but also come close to shore where they sit on rocks and preen themselves. Celtic legends say they can also be found in marshes and fens, and European tales claim merfolk reside in rivers, lakes, and waterfalls. Like their water-spirit predecessors, mermaids seem at home in freshwater as well as the salty seas.

In his 3,000-year-old epic *Theogony*, the poet Hesiod wrote that the Greek merman Triton and his parents, Poseidon and Amphitrite, lived in a golden palace at the bottom of the sea. Some legends say mermaids make their homes in coral caves in the ocean's depths. Other tales suggest that mermaids inhabit the long-lost continents of Atlantis and Lemuria, which supposedly sank to the ocean floors eons ago.

Published in 1891, *The Folk-Lore of the Isle of Man*, by A. W. Moore, stated that the people of the Isle of Man believed "a splendid city, with many towers and gilded minarets, once stood near Langness, on a spot now covered by the sea." Here, merfolk dwelt, surrounded by treasure they'd accumulated from the ships they'd caused to sink.

Considering that people all over the world have reported seeing mermaids in all sorts of environments and locations, we can assume these mysterious and versatile creatures are capable of living almost anywhere—even on land, at least for a while. Ultimately, though, they reject the land-based lives they've embarked on and return to their true home: the sea.

Siren Sightings

In the 1600s, Renaissance entrepreneurs decided to plumb the underwater realms off the Isle of Man by lowering a man encased in a glass bubble-like device into the depths. The explorers hoped to make a fortune by recovering sunken treasure they believed lay hidden beneath the sea. However, they ran out of rope before their man reached the bottom. When his companions pulled him back up, he reported having witnessed an underwater paradise with streets made of coral, glistening pyramids of crystal, and mother-of-pearl buildings decorated with colorful shells. He described one room he managed to observe closely as being constructed of precious stones of all kinds. Additionally, he claimed to have met "comely mermen and beautiful mermaids, the inhabitants of this blissful realm."

FINFOLKAHEEM

Orkney Islanders speak of a place called Finfolkaheem meaning "the finfolk's home" as a wondrous palace built on the ocean floor and surrounded by seaweed gardens. Its grand rooms and hallways are reportedly made of crystal and illuminated by blue-green phosphorescence, which plankton and creatures that live in the deep naturally give off.

Elusive Beauties

ctually, countless people claim they've seen mermaids and mermen. Some even insist they've had close encounters with these gorgeous girls and guys. And yet, despite the frequency with which merfolk show up, we have no hard proof of their validity—no bones, no fins, only some whacky pictures and some monstrous phonies.

As you've learned, old legends and lore speak of mermaids and other hybrid creatures as having lived on the earth, just like humans and animals. In many of those folktales, mermaids even married people and produced children. These seafolk could change shape at will, turning in their fishtails for legs temporarily, so they could walk on land. But some contemporary researchers believe that not only can mermaids magically shapeshift from human beings to fish or reptiles, they also can transform themselves from physical to nonphysical entities. Like the spirit animals of Native

American mythology, merfolk can move between the material and spirit worlds with a flip of their fishtails. The only time we can see them is when we are on the same wavelength, so to speak—like fairies and angels.

We have no way of knowing whether mermaids present themselves to humans more often now than they did in ancient times, but one thing is certain. Their likenesses are omnipresent, enticing us from retail stores, catalogs, online sites, and even Las Vegas shows. And it's a safe bet that mermaids will continue to live among us for the foreseeable future.

MERMAID FANTASY GAMES

People who love fantasy games can play with the merfolk by visiting the online game site mythara.wikia.com. The site explains merfolk's culture, social relations, economy, politics, religion, and more—at least from the perspective of Mythara's creators and players.

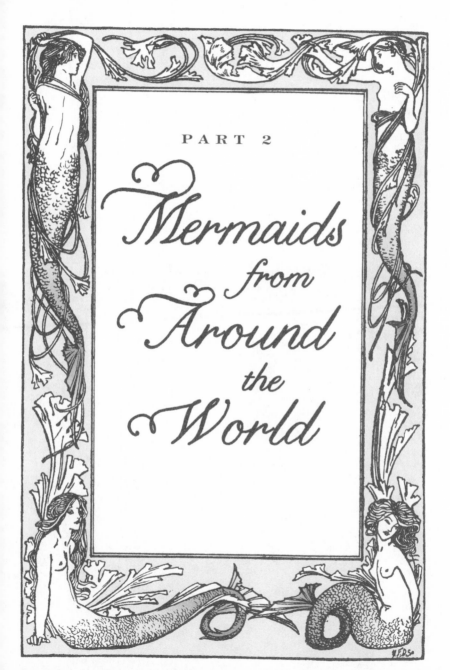

PART 2

Mermaids from Around the World

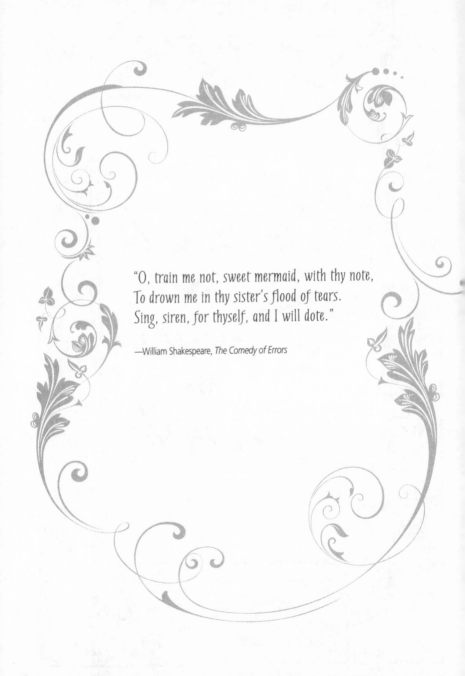

"O, train me not, sweet mermaid, with thy note,
To drown me in thy sister's flood of tears.
Sing, siren, for thyself, and I will dote."

—William Shakespeare, *The Comedy of Errors*

CHAPTER 4

Mermaids OF THE Ancient World

IF WE ARE TO BELIEVE the many legends of the world, merfolk swam through the waters of our planet long before recorded history, where they fascinated the ancients—just as they do modern people today. Like the earliest human civilizations, the earliest mermaid myths come from Mesopotamia, and date back several thousand years.

Virtually all ancient cultures give accounts of strange, hybrid aquatic creatures, some of them considered divine in nature. At a time when spirits of all kinds populated the universe and the world was a mysterious place, our ancestors believed that potent deities controlled the great oceans and mighty rivers. Many of the myths of these cultures overlap or bear similarities, as do their deities. Centuries of trade, war, and migration facilitated the exchange of ideas in the ancient world, as still happens today, merging foreign concepts with indigenous beliefs to create a colorful blend of legends and lore.

Assyria—Birthplace of the Mermaid

ermaid researchers say our first real mermaid came from Assyria (Syria). According to myth, the ancient Assyrians worshiped Atargatis, a powerful moon and fertility goddess, and associated her with life-giving water.

Mythology connects both the moon and water with the dark, mysterious, and ever-changing nature of women. Early people both revered and feared their female deities. These qualities, which people throughout the ages have associated with mermaids, may have originated with Atargatis—the goddess-turned-mermaid who threw herself into a lake after her catastrophic tryst with a shepherd (see Chapter 1)—and continue to this day.

In the first century C.E., Syrian writer Lucian described Atargatis's temple in the city of Ascalon on the Mediterranean as being richly appointed, with a gold ceiling and doors. The temple held a golden statue of her, covered with gemstones, and another of her consort, the god Hadad. A sacred lake near the temple was filled with pampered fish. An altar sat in the middle of the lake, and worshippers could swim to it if they wanted to make offerings to the goddess.

Atargatis's fame spread to Greece and Rome, and eventually through Europe and Britain as the Romans traversed the continent, bringing her legend with them. The Greeks called her Derketo, the Romans Dea Syria, meaning "the Syrian Goddess."

THE BIRTH OF THE
CONSTELLATION PISCES

A Greek story says that long ago an egg fell from the sky into the Euphrates River. A fish pushed the egg to shore and Derketo (the Greek name for Atargatis) hatched from it. She asked Zeus to acknowledge the fish's help by forming the constellation Pisces, the zodiac sign represented by two fish. Ever after, fish were sacred to her.

Babylonian Water Divinities

 ne of the greatest of the ancient water deities was the Babylonian goddess Tiamat. Mythology honors this dragon-goddess and her consort, Apsu, as the parents of all the other Babylonian deities. Tiamat, it's said, even created the Tigris and Euphrates rivers. When her murderous son Marduk cut her in half, the two rivers gushed from her eyes.

According to Thorkild Jacobsen, former professor of Assyriology at Harvard University and author of *The Sumerian Kinglist*, in the beginning "all was a watery chaos." Two primal forces, Tiamat (the sea) and Apsu (the fresh water that existed underground), mingled and created the other gods and goddesses. "They engendered the god of heaven, Anu, and he in turn the god of the flowing sweet waters, Ea."

The ancient Babylonians believed the Earth floated on fresh water. Ea, the god of wisdom, art, farming, and building, was also considered the ruler of these primal waters. Some images show him as a merman, with a human torso and the tail of a fish. When Ea wanted to teach knowledge to humankind, he sent the Apkulla—wise beings who supposedly had existed from the beginning of time—to carry out the task. Some of these sages appeared as human-bird composites. Others dressed in the skins of fish.

When the Babylonians wanted to "sign" documents, they used sealstones—stones carved with their personal emblems—and pressed them into hot wax as seals. One sealstone dating back to the eighteenth century B.C.E. shows a half-human half-fish creature—the earliest-known depiction of a mermaid.

MARINE BIOLOGIST OR MERMAID?

In the 1983 movie *Local Hero*, a Texas oil company wants to buy an entire Scottish village as a site for a refinery. The film features an unusual character named Marina, which means "watery area." A marine biologist, she has webbed toes and appears to live in the sea. Marina is also the name of the little mermaid in Hans Christian Andersen's fairy tale.

Sumerian Water Deities

eities of all kinds populated ancient Sumer (Sumeria) as well as Assyria and Babylonia. Gods and goddesses governed every facet of Mesopotamian life—they even ruled the Tigris and the Euphrates rivers between which these city-states lay. Sumerian divinities included numerous human-animal hybrids—some benevolent and some malevolent—from whom researchers believe mermaids may have evolved. These include not only the familiar fishtailed creatures we commonly think of as merfolk, but also humans with fish heads or fish-shaped hoods, people dressed in scaly garments, and men with fish skins draped on their backs.

One of ancient Sumer's most important deities was a sea goddess named Nammu who birthed humankind. They thought of her as the goddess of the primeval sea, the mother of heaven and Earth—the Primordial Mother.

The Sumerians also honored a water god, Enki, who was their equivalent of Babylon's god Ea. Known as the lord of water and wisdom, Enki was sometimes pictured in early artwork with water flowing from his shoulders. He also has ties to the serpent deities found in other cultures—his symbol, much like the caduceus adopted by doctors as their emblem, showed two serpents wrapped around a staff. We even find parallels between Enki and Noah, the man who built the ark in Christian mythology. In Sumerian mythology, Enki taught a man named Ziusudra to build a boat that would save human beings during the flood.

A SPLASH OF ENLIGHTENMENT

When it came time for people to leave their primitive ways behind, Sumerian myths say a mermaid emerged from the ocean to educate humanity in social, scientific, and artistic areas.

The Arabian Nights

magine the beautiful Scheherazade thousands of years ago delighting the Persian king Shahryah with magical tales of mermaids. The stories she tells in *One Thousand and One Nights* (known as *The Arabian Nights* in the English-speaking world) explore fantastic and fanciful worlds where anything can, and does, occur. Here we find familiar accounts of mermaids who bedazzle sailors with their glorious singing, and then either drown or devour the helpless men. But many other merfolk and water deities also play starring roles in these tales.

The Adventures of Bulukiya

One of the 1001 stories in this beloved compilation, this tale features a seafarer who comes upon whole societies of mermaids while searching for an herb that will confer immortality.

Djullanar the Sea-girl

This tale describes sea people who, although anatomically human, lived in the underwater realms. They married earthly humans and produced offspring who could breathe underwater.

Abdullah the Fisherman and Abdullah the Merman

In this story a fisherman who goes to live underwater discovers a world with practices and values that are entirely different from those on Earth, and where the inhabitants don't wear clothes or work.

Julnar the Sea-Born and Her Son King Badr Basim of Persia

Here a king falls in love with a beautiful sea-born creature who tells him she and her kind "walk in the waters with our eyes open, as do ye on the ground."

This fascinating collection of stories, drawn from Arabic, Persian, Turkish, Egyptian, and Indian folklore over a period of many centuries, shows how from antiquity merfolk sparked the imaginations of diverse populations—just as they do today.

MAIL A MERMAID

Mermaids make colorful subjects for postage stamps. A picture of a selkie female with her captor appears on a Faroese 5.50 KR stamp. The English 90p stamp features a blue mermaid, modestly covering her breasts. In Australia, a mermaid by artist Aaron Lee Pocock graces the 60c stamp.

The Nubile Nymphs of Greece

"According to the philosophers of antiquity, every fountain had its nymph; every ocean wave its oceanid. The water spirits were known under such names as oreades, nereides, limoniades, naiades, water sprites, sea maids, mermaids, and potamides."

—Manly P. Hall, *The Secret Teachings of All Ages*

ultures have a way of assuming the myths of others and adapting various deities to suit their own needs. Consequently, many Greek deities have Roman counterparts. The Greeks and Romans also co-opted gods and goddesses from other countries and shoe-horned these divinities into their own pantheons. Characteristics of Assyria's Atargatis, for example, can easily been seen in the Greek's Aphrodite and the Roman's Venus.

We don't find many mermaids in Greek and Roman myths, but we do encounter plenty of water nymphs, who comprised a group of minor aquatic deities. Nereus (a sea god) and Doris (a nymph) had fifty nymph daughters, known collectively as the nereids. The Greeks and Romans, it seems, eschewed the powerful, tempestuous, life-and-death-giving goddesses that many other cultures worshiped, preferring the sweetly seductive, nubile nymphs instead.

As discussed in Chapter 1, the Greeks categorized the nymphs according to their environments. Naiads (from the Greek word for running water) lived in flowing freshwater: streams, springs, and fountains. The oceanids made their homes in the oceans, and the nereids (also saltwater spirits) dwelt in the seas, primarily the Mediterranean, Adriatic, and Aegean, which surround Greece. These lovely water spirits, despite their lack of fishy attributes, may have served as inspirations for mermaids.

TEMPESTUOUS THESSALONIKE

Alexander the Great's sister Thessalonike (for whom the Greek city was named) supposedly transformed into a mermaid after her death. As a mermaid, she appeared to seamen and asked, "Does Alexander the Great live?" If sailors gave the wrong answer, Thessalonike whipped up ferocious storms to punish them. If they answered correctly, however, she spared them. The correct response was "He lives and reigns and conquers the world."

Greek Water Gods and Goddesses

hat about male water spirits in Greek mythology? Actually, quite a few male deities with fishy and/or snaky tails ruled the waters of ancient Greece—let's meet a few of them.

The powerful serpent-like river god Oceanus was so enormous he encircled the globe. He and his wife, Tethys, created the rivers of the world—3,000 of them. The Greeks also had their version of the Babylonian's merman water god, Ea, whom they called

Oannes. Most important to the story of mermaids, though, is the river god Achelous, for whom Greece's largest river is named. It was Achelous, the son of Oceanus and Tethys, who fathered the infamous temptresses, the Sirens.

When it comes to water spirits, Greek mythology had its bad guys as well as its good guys. Greek folklore contained lots of scary water monsters. Typhon, a huge and terrifying beast, combined a man's body with a serpent's tail. The goddess Ceto governed the perils of the sea, including aquatic beasts such as sharks, killer whales, and sea monsters that threatened early seafarers. She and her husband Phorcys produced numerous children known collectively as the Phorcydes—some nice, some nasty. The "nice girls" included the Hesperides (nymphs) and the Graeae (water goddesses). Among the "bad girls" were Medusa and the infamous gorgons, who had poisonous snakes sprouting from their heads instead of hair, and the terrifying Scylla, who gobbled up six of Odysseus's seamen. Over time, the name "Ceto" became synonymous with sea monster.

FROM MER TO MAN

In the fifth century B.C.E., the noted pre-Socratic philosopher Anaximander of Miletus postulated that humans evolved from merfolk.

Triton: The Best-Known Merman of Them All

 he best known of all Greco-Roman water gods is Triton, son of Poseidon (Neptune to the Romans) and Amphitrite, who ruled the ancient seas. Myth says they all lived together in a magnificent golden palace beneath the seas. Although his parents didn't have fishtails themselves, Triton did. Sometimes artwork even shows him with not just one but two tails—and occasionally with two legs *and* a fishtail. The Roman poet Ovid described him as "sea-hued" with "shoulders barnacled with sea-shells."

Triton is often depicted blowing a curly conch shell, as he is in Bernini's famous Roman fountain, and his music was said to control the seas. In ancient times, people followed the merman's lead and blew the spiral-shaped shells of large sea snails known as Tritons or Triton trumpets.

Triton spawned a whole family of fish-guys called the Tritons— and a few fish-girls known as Tritonids or Tritonesses. The males of the species, according to second-century geographer Pausanius, had torsos covered with fine, shark-like scales, human-like faces and hands, and tails similar to a dolphin's.

The Tritons served as escorts for Aphrodite. This sea-born goddess (the Greek's equivalent of Venus) presided over smooth sailing and, naturally, mariners loved her. Often she appears in art and literature with a dolphin as a companion. This gives her a "fish" connection, even though Aphrodite herself had a fully human body. Botticelli's famous painting places the goddess on a huge scallop shell, another link to sea creatures.

MERMEN IN THE SKY?

Triton is the largest moon of the planet Neptune. The sea god Neptune, for whom the planet was named in 1846, is the Roman version of the Greek's Poseidon, Triton's father.

MERMEN MASCOTS

Even if you didn't know about this famous Greco-Roman merman before, you've probably heard Triton's name. A number of athletic teams have adopted him as their symbol, including the University of California, San Diego, and the University of Missouri, St. Louis.

The Sirens

"On Greek vases or Roman murals [the Sirens] appear as bird-women, sometimes just with human heads, sometimes human to the waist so that they have arms with which to play musical instruments."

—Gail-Nina Anderson, "Mermaids in Myth and Art," *www.forteantimes.com*

 he term "sirens" has become synonymous with dangerously beguiling women as well as mermaids. But the original Sirens weren't mermaids at all. Rather, they combined the features of women and birds.

Myth says these daughters of the Greek river god Achelous had such enchantingly beautiful voices that seafarers who heard them became delirious with delight—and either smashed their ships onto rocks or jumped overboard and drowned. According to legend, the Sirens also played musical instruments, which could be why we often see pictures of mermaids holding lutes or flutes.

The Sirens' best-known role in ancient literature is in Homer's epic poem *Odyssey*, where they attempt to lure the hero Odysseus to his death. However, Homer doesn't describe these beautiful beasties as possessing aquatic characteristics.

Not until the rise of Christianity did the Sirens begin to relinquish their feathers in favor of fishtails. Some researchers speculate that this shift occurred because Christian art and literature associated wings with angels and the church fathers wanted to avoid confusion. After all, the Sirens were dangerous temptresses, symbolizing the concept of feminine seduction and evil that began with

Eve. Thus, it seemed better to give them fishy or snakelike appendages that recalled the serpent in the Garden of Eden and, not coin-
cidentally, obscured their reproductive organs.

Carved in stone, Sirens and mermaids decorate many medieval
Christian churches, including France's Notre Dame de Cunault
and England's St. Laurence, Ludlow (Shropshire). Early illuminated manuscripts also used Sirens to illustrate their pages—and
depicted them as the beautiful, bare-breasted mermaids we know
and love today.

Siren Sightings

In a Greek legend, a fisherman named Glaucus
started out as a human being. However, he
became a merman after eating what he believed
to be enchanted grass that he thought had
brought some fish he'd caught back to life. Feeling
irresistibly drawn to the sea, Glaucus dove in, and
the sea deities transformed his legs into a fishtail.
The Roman poet Ovid recounts Glaucus's story in
Metamorphoses.

"It was rather annoying to Jack that, though living in a place where the merrows were as plenty as lobsters, he never could get a right view of one."

—William Butler Yeats, *Irish Folk Stories and Fairy Tales*

CHAPTER 5

Mermaids OF THE British Isles AND Ireland

MORE THAN 3 MILLION PEOPLE make their homes along the United Kingdom's coastline of nearly 20,000 miles, and people who live near the sea always swap stories about mermaids. Ireland—a country known for its fairies, leprechauns, and other mythical beings—has its share of mermaid legends as well. In fact, the UK Travel Bureau touts Britain and Ireland as "THE spiritual home of ancient Myths, Magic and Legends." Colorful tales of aquatic folk also come from the Isle of Man, the Faroes, Orkneys, Shetlands, and Britain's other islands. Mermaids even captured the imaginations of Shakespeare, Chaucer, Donne, Yeats, and other literary giants. What's so alluring about these countries' merfolk? Read on!

The Selkies

n many parts of Scotland, England, and Ireland tales are told of a mysterious race of beings known as the selkies. The term comes from the Scottish word *selch* for seal. According to legend, the selkies or "seal wives" don the skins of seals that let them navigate the waters surrounding Britain and Ireland. When they decide to come ashore, they remove their sealskins and shapeshift into human beings—men as well as women, for both sexes exist among the selkies.

Like mermaids, these aquatic creatures can breathe underwater and the ocean is their true home. Welsh legend suggests that selkies were actually born human, but soon after birth they chose to live in the ocean instead of on land. Selkie females are reputed to be irresistibly beautiful, with tantalizing voices.

Unlike merfolk of other cultures, these comely creatures don't usually harm human beings. Fishermen consider them good luck and seeing a selkie can mean a bountiful catch. Most selkies only stay on land for short periods of time and establish close, personal connections with only one human at a time. Often that person—even if he's married to a selkie—doesn't realize his mate's true identity. Selkies

must keep their sealskins safely hidden while on land, for without their magic pelts the selkies can't return to the sea.

Some people believe they descended from the selkies. A Scottish legend says the MacCodrum clan fell into this group. Known in Gaelic as Clann Mhic Codruim nan rón (Clan MacCodrum of the seals), the family supposedly lived as seals during the day and shapeshifted into human beings at night.

LONDON'S MERMAID TAVERN

Founded in the fifteenth century, the famous Mermaid Tavern on London's Bread Street was a favorite hangout for prominent Elizabethan gentlemen. A literary club met there in the early 1600s; members included such luminaries as Ben Jonson and Francis Beaumont. A painting by Faed called *Shakespeare and His Contemporaries* pictures the Bard at the Mermaid Tavern with his friends Sir Walter Raleigh, John Donne, Francis Bacon, and the Earl of Southampton.

Selkie Stories

any selkie legends end tragically, such as *The Secret of Roan Inish* (a 1994 film directed by John Sayles, based on Rosalie K. Fry's novel *The Secret of the Ron Mor Skerry*, discussed in Chapter 2). In the old Orkney Islands ballad, the "Great Silkie of Sule Skerry," a selkie male has a child with a human woman. The selkie comes to claim his son, and in exchange gives the mother a purse full of gold. Before they depart, the selkie predicts a sad fate for himself and the child—for selkies are known to possess the gift of clairvoyance. He tells the woman that she'll marry a gunner who will kill both her son and the selkie father.

In a tale from the Shetland Islands, a seal hunter named Herman Perk becomes stranded during a storm. A selkie male rescues him after making Perk promise to return the selkie's wife's pelt, which had been stolen, so she can change back into a seal and rejoin him in the sea.

Another story tells of a selkie's revenge on the residents of the Kalsoy Island in the Faroes because the men killed her seal husband and children. The selkie swears to drown the people or cause them to fall from cliffs until so many have died that their ghosts could hold hands and encircle the island.

SOULS OF THE DROWNED

Some folklore tells us that the selkies developed from the souls of humans who drowned at sea—they're magical and mystical beings.

The Merrow

rish folklore describes a gentle and benevolent race of merfolk called the merrow. The word comes from the Gaelic *murúch* or *muiroighe—muir* means "sea" and *oigh* means "young woman." Like mermaids from other cultures, merrows combine beautiful human torsos with fishy lower parts—at least when they live in the ocean. However, legend says these lovely beings—males as well as females—occasionally assume legs and come ashore for long periods of time. There they mingle with and marry human beings, even raise families. Despite their wondrous singing voices and webbed fingers, their loved ones and neighbors may not realize their true identities. In the end, though, merrow-folk long for their watery home and usually return to the sea.

One peculiarity of the merrows is the *cohuleen druith*, a magical red hat that gives them the ability to live underwater. This special talisman serves a purpose similar to that of the selkie's sealskin—for if a merrow loses her precious hat, she can't return to her underwater world.

Another unique quality of the merrow is her pleasant disposition—she seems to lack the tempestuous and sometimes malicious nature expressed by mermaids from other locales. Although lady merrows have been known to tempt human men into their aquatic realms, legend says those males lived happily ever after with their mermaid mates. They even became merfolk themselves and shared the merrows' enchanted existence beneath the sea.

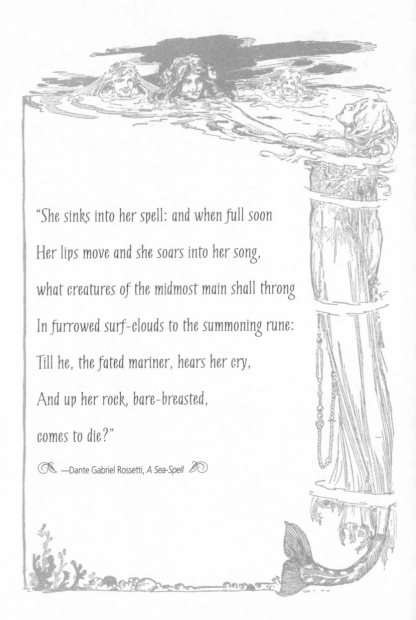

"She sinks into her spell: and when full soon

Her lips move and she soars into her song,

what creatures of the midmost main shall throng

In furrowed surf-clouds to the summoning rune:

Till he, the fated mariner, hears her cry,

And up her rock, bare-breasted,

comes to die?"

—Dante Gabriel Rossetti, *A Sea-Spell*

MARRIED TO A MERMAID

Irish sailors who drowned at sea were said to have "married a mermaid."

The Merry Maids of Cornwall

 teeped in mythology and folklore, Cornwall lies at the center of England's most beloved and enduring legend, that of King Arthur. Not surprisingly, plenty of mermaid stories and sightings also come from this seaside locale. Cornish mermaids—or "merry maids"—share many characteristics of mermaids elsewhere: great beauty, enchanting singing voices, and a penchant for luring mariners to watery graves.

Reputedly, mermaids comb their hair and enchant Cornish fishermen at a place known as Mermaid's Rock near Lamorna on Cornwall's eastern tip. Legend says that if the mermaids are heard singing, a ship will sink nearby seven days later.

Despite their name, the merry maids aren't always cheerful. According to one Cornish story, an angry merry maid took revenge on the town of Padstow, transforming its waterway from a thriving port into a treacherous sandbar ominously known as Doom Bar. Once the seafarers' helpful friend, the mermaid used to sit on a rock in the town's cove and she guided large ships up the River Camel safely into the harbor. Then one day a sailor shot her— stories vary as to who killed her and why—and with her dying breath she cursed the town. Never again would ships sail into Padstow's harbor, she swore.

Soon a storm arose, destroying a number of craft in the area. In the river's mouth the turbulent tides deposited a huge mass of sand on which ships foundered. The once navigable waters became so shallow that only small boats could make their way into Padstow, and over the centuries many ships wrecked on Doom Bar. The mermaid's curse prevailed.

DIVINE ANCESTRY

Some Irish say that before human beings occupied the Emerald Isle, a race of semi-divine beings lived there. These deities may have resembled mermaids, and some Irish families believe they are descended from these mythical beings.

The Mermaid of Zennor

n old Cornish tale gives a different spin to the familiar idea of mermaids enchanting men with their songs. In this story, a strange, lovely, and well-dressed woman became enthralled with a handsome young Zennor man named Mathew Trewella, known throughout the village for his magnificent singing voice, and she came to hear him sing in church. Attracted by her beauty and mysterious nature, Mathew decided to get to know the woman. One Sunday after church, he followed her as she walked to the cliffs overlooking the sea—but he never returned.

Years later, a ship's captain weighed anchor near Zennor and soon a mermaid hailed him with her charming voice. She asked him to lift his anchor, for it lay on the roof of her underwater abode where she lived with Mathew Trewella. The mermaid, named Morveren, the daughter of the sea king Llyr, turned out to be the beautiful woman who'd come ashore to hear Mathew sing. Zennor's fishermen still hear Mathew's voice soaring on the waves. If he sings high, they say, the seas will be smooth, but it'll be rough going if he sings low.

WARNING TO THE FAITHFUL

In a sixteenth-century church on the northern coast of Cornwall near St. Ives, the end panel of a wooden pew features a handsome carving of a typical mermaid. The *bas relief* figure, dubbed the Mermaid of Zennor, holds a mirror in one hand and a comb in the other. Is she a symbol of good luck to the local fishermen? Or, does she warn the faithful against sins of the flesh, like mermaid depictions in many medieval Christian churches?

Wise and Winsome Wishes

ike fairies, leprechauns, and genies, mermaids are said to have the ability to grant wishes and bring good luck to human beings. These wise and winsome creatures have been known to share the gift of knowledge with humans, to heal the sick, and to offer treasures of all kinds to people they favor. If you capture a mermaid, she may share a secret with you or give you a reward in exchange for her freedom. But magical merfolk can be tricksters, and their gifts often come with strings attached.

According to Cornish myth, a fisherman named Lutey Cury rescues a beached mermaid and helps her back into the water. In return, she promises him three wishes. He asks her for the power to heal the sick, the power to defuse wicked spells, and to have these powers passed on to his children after his death. The mermaid grants his wishes, but then tries to drag Lutey into the sea with her. Knowing that iron is an amulet against the dangers of mermaids and other supernatural beings, he pulls out his knife and escapes.

For nine years, Lutey uses his gifts for the good of the Cornish people. But at the end of that time, the mermaid returns to take Lutey back with her to her home beneath the sea. After his disappearance, Lutey's children receive his powers according to his third wish. But Lutey's good fortune comes at a high price. In return for the mermaid's largess, every nine years the sea claims one of Lutey's descendants.

HARRY POTTER MEETS
THE MERFOLK

Merpeople attend the funeral of wizard Albus Dumbledore in *Harry Potter and the Half-Blood Prince*, the sixth novel in J. K. Rowling's popular series. Unlike the beautiful merfolk in most folklore, these beasts are things only a mother could love, with gray skin on their upper humanoid torsos and silver fishtails, green hair and beards, yellow eyes, and broken yellow teeth. When they speak, they screech instead of enchanting people with melodious songs—for ostensibly their language is intended to be heard underwater.

The Blue Men of the Muir

lthough females dominate merfolk mythology, Scottish folklore includes a group of mermen known as the Blue Men of the Muir. *Muir* is the Gaelic word for "sea." Named for their blue-gray color, these dangerous water spirits—like Alexander the Great's mermaid sister Thessalonike (see Chapter 4)—approached mariners and asked them a question. If the seamen couldn't answer it correctly, the mermen wrecked their ships and dragged the sailors down into the depths.

The Blue Men were said to live in the Minch Channel, a body of water between the western islands of the Hebrides, off the coast of northern Scotland. Generations of sailors and fishermen have reported seeing these sea-colored merfolk riding the waves near the Shiant Islands. Shiant means "charmed" and the Blue Men are believed to be magical spirits who cause the turbulent tides there. Struth nan Fear Gorma, a body of water between the Shiant Islands and the Isle of Lewis, means "the Stream of the Blue Men."

Other Scottish legends tell of dark, dangerous merfolk who reside in the waters near the Orkney Islands. Known as the Finfolk, these mysterious and malevolent beings normally live under the sea in a place called Finfolkaheem, but swim or steal boats to come ashore. Looking for human captives, the Finfolk wait for unsupervised children who stray near the water and nab them—then they take their captives to Finfolkaheem and keep them there as slaves.

GREEDY MERMEN

Scottish legend says the Finfolk are fond of silver, especially silver jewelry. If you ever find yourself endangered by one of these creatures, toss three silver coins as far away from you as possible. The greedy beast will drop you and scurry after the money.

Ladies of the Lakes

reland and Britain's mermaids not only swim through the salty seas, they also make their homes in freshwater. Some of these mystical maids are believed to have divine lineages. Others possess more sinister natures.

One such malevolent mermaid appears in the Mermaids' Pool below Kinder Downfall in Derbyshire each year on Easter's Eve at the stroke of midnight. Legend says that if you lean over to gaze into the pool, you may see a vision of the future—or the mermaid may drag you down to your death. Another mermaid haunts Black Mere Pool near Leek in the North Staffordshire Moors, according to local folklore. A number people have drowned in this eerie spot, and in 1679 a serial killer dumped a female victim's body in the pool. Perhaps that's why the mermaid supposedly rises from the dark pool at midnight to reap vengeance by enticing unwitting male passersby to their deaths.

Celtic goddesses often appear as triparted beings, representing the three phases of womanhood: maiden, mother, and crone. In her maiden form, the Irish lake goddess Aine is depicted as a mermaid, reputed to live at the bottom of Ireland's Lough Gur. Legend says the Earl of Desmond captured her by stealing her magic cloak (a garment similar to the selkie's sealskin), and they had a son together. After the child's birth, the Earl granted Aine her freedom and she returned to the lake. Years later, their son joined her there.

Every seven years, Lough Gur supposedly dries up. When this happens, you can see a sacred tree (perhaps the Celtic World Tree) growing in the bottom of the lake, where Aine in her crone-form lives and knits the cloth of life.

THE MERMAID INN

In the mid-nineteenth century a pub near Black Mere Pool capitalized on the legend and renamed itself the Mermaid Inn. It claims to be the highest-elevation restaurant in England, sited on a hill 1,640 feet above sea level.

Water Fairies

*"This mysterious female gave Arthur his sword Excalibur . . .
She may be a Celtic lake divinity in origin, perhaps of the same kind
as the Gwagged Annwn—lake fairies in modern Welsh folklore."*

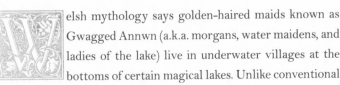

—Ronan Coghlan, *The Illustrated Encyclopaedia of Arthurian Legends*

elsh mythology says golden-haired maids known as Gwagged Annwn (a.k.a. morgans, water maidens, and ladies of the lake) live in underwater villages at the bottoms of certain magical lakes. Unlike conventional mermaids, these water fairies lack the usual fishy features—they appear completely human. These lovely creatures not only swim in the lakes of Wales, they can sometimes be seen walking weightlessly on the surface of the water or gliding along in golden boats.

Just as mermaids and other sea deities do, the Gwagged Annwn sometimes mingle with people, coming on land to take human lovers. The fairies call the shots, however, and if their mates don't adhere to the rules set by these beautiful water maids they disappear, back into their underwater homes.

Another type of water fairy known as the asrai (also called Dancers on the Mist and scarille) hide underwater during the day—but at night they can sometimes be seen dancing on the surface of ponds and lakes. Some people say they resemble mist. If sunlight hits them, the asrai melt into the water and disappear.

Like mermaids, their haunting beauty enchants men. Legends describe them as having pale, silvery skin and the bodies of comely young women that don't deteriorate, even though the asrai can live to be hundreds of years old. But don't get too close to these mysterious maids—their touch is like dry ice and it can burn your skin instantly. Usually believed to inhabit the lakes and rivers of Shropshire and Cheshire, England, the asrai have been known to show up in Scotland's waters, too.

MERMAID MUSES

Merfolk have populated the Emerald Isle's waters for millennia, serving as subjects for numerous Irish bards. They go by other Gaelic names as well, including *Muir-gheilt*, *Samhghubha*, *Muidhuachán*, and *Suire*. The *Suire*, a type of sea nymph, supposedly greeted the Milesians when they first landed in Ireland.

Captured Mermaids

ccasionally, someone manages to capture a mermaid. The *Annals of Ulster* and the *Annals of the Kingdom of Ireland by the Four Masters* (which chronicle Celtic history) list several accounts of mermaids who were caught in the years 558, 571, 887, and 1118. The 887 entry in *Annals of the Four Masters* is most unusual. It reported that a huge mermaid washed up on the Scottish coast—a pure white creature 195 feet long with hair 18 feet long and fingers 7 feet long!

In 1810, three men claimed to have discovered two merchildren on the Isle of Man. One had died, but the other had a brown body about two feet long with a scaly purple tail and green hair. In Suffolk, during the twelfth century, locals trapped a merman and imprisoned him in Orford Castle for six months until he finally managed to escape.

A popular Irish legend tells of a girl named Liban or Lioth Bean (meaning "beautiful woman") whose family died in a flood. She survived by metamorphosing into a half-human, half-salmon mermaid and went to live in an underwater cave. Like other mer-

maids, she possessed an exquisite singing voice and the people of Ulster became so enamored of her that they decided to capture her. Even the local cleric couldn't resist Liban's charms—he insisted that she be buried with him in the same casket. To smooth over the awkward situation, the church canonized her as St. Murgen (meaning sea-born). She now serves as the spiritual guardian of Ulster.

PIRATES AND MERMAIDS

In *Pirates of the Caribbean: On Stranger Tides*, the notorious English pirate Blackbeard and his crew set out to capture a mermaid in a place called Whitecap Bay, where mermaids are believed to thrive. Several seamen use themselves as "bait" to attract the sultry sirens—but the mermaids turn out to be more than a match for the sailors. A battle ensues and the sea maids sink the pirates' ship. But some of the men manage to capture a sweet and beautiful young mermaid named Syrena. As mermaids sometimes do, she falls in love with one of the crew, a missionary named Philip Swift, and spirits him away to live with her in the sea.

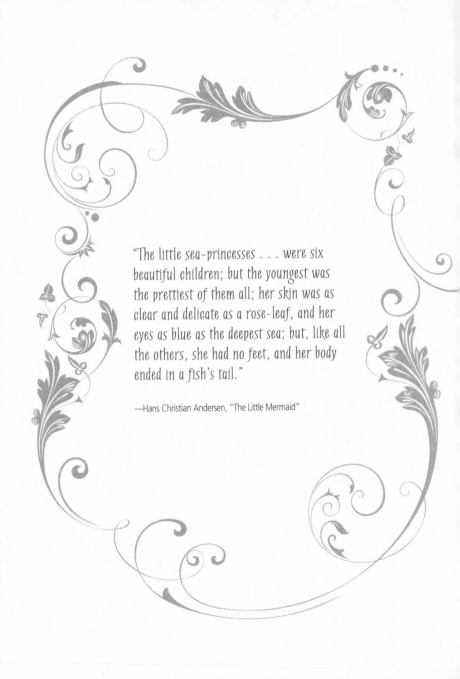

"The little sea-princesses . . . were six
beautiful children; but the youngest was
the prettiest of them all; her skin was as
clear and delicate as a rose-leaf, and her
eyes as blue as the deepest sea; but, like all
the others, she had no feet, and her body
ended in a fish's tail."

—Hans Christian Andersen, "The Little Mermaid"

CHAPTER 6

European Mermaids

EUROPE'S MERFOLK are as interesting and diverse as the people who populate this continent. Some, including Scandinavia's handsome Havman and Warsaw's benevolent protectress Warszawska Syrenka, are usually friendly toward humans. Others, such as Germany's nix, display the merfolk's darker side. The most famous of all—and perhaps the most beloved today—hails from Denmark: Hans Christian Andersen's little mermaid.

The Story of the Little Mermaid

ur modern-day fascination with mermaids stems, in large part, from Disney's movie version of Hans Christian Andersen's fairy tale, "The Little Mermaid." Released in 1989, the film won two Oscars and two Golden Globe awards, and has become one of the most celebrated animated movies of all time.

In Disney's version of the story, a curious young mermaid named Ariel wants to leave her family's underwater paradise and visit the world of humans. Against the wishes of her father, King Triton, she surfaces one night and rescues Prince Eric after his

boat sinks in a storm. She drags him to shore and sings to him. In time, the pair fall in love, and after a number of complications and confrontations with a scheming contender for Triton's throne, the little mermaid's father transforms her into a human so she can marry the prince.

The original 1836 story is much darker, however, and the movie, in order to make it more appealing to little girls, takes many liberties with the fairy tale's interpretation. In Andersen's story, a fifteen-year-old mermaid named Marina wants to gain an immortal soul, which many myths say can only happen if the mermaid marries a human man. A sea witch gives Marina a magic potion to drink that turns her into a two-legged being—but in the bargain she must suffer great pain each time she takes a step, have her tongue cut out, and sacrifice her beautiful voice. Marina falls in love with the prince and goes to live on land as his dear friend. But he ends up marrying another woman, depriving the broken-hearted former mermaid of an immortal soul, life as a human, and the possibility of returning to the sea as a mermaid.

A NYMPH AND A NOVELLA

The novella *Undine*, written by French author Friedrich de la Motte Fouqué in 1811, tells the story of a water nymph named Undine who wants to marry a human prince. *Undine* achieved international success and was made into both an opera and a ballet. It may also have inspired Andersen's fairy tale a quarter-century later.

Copenhagen's Little Mermaid

ach year, more than a million people visit Copenhagen's biggest tourist attraction: the statue of the Little Mermaid, *Den Lille Havfrue*. One of the world's most popular beauties, the bronze statue was given to the city of Copenhagen—Hans Christian Andersen's birthplace—by Carl Jacobsen of Carlsberg Breweries. She took up residence in her current spot in the harbor near Langelinie Pier on August 23, 1913, a time when the city chose to adorn its public areas with figures from history and mythology.

Inspired by dancer Ellen Price's performance in the ballet "The Little Mermaid" at the Royal Theatre in 1909, Jacobsen hired a little-known sculptor, Edvard Erichsen, to create the statue. Price modeled for the mermaid's head, but Erichsen's wife took over when it came time for the sculptor to fashion the figure's nude body. The seated statue is a little over 4 feet high and weighs about 386 pounds. The sculptor depicted Den Lille Havfrue with legs as well as a fishtail and positioned her looking out over the water, apparently remembering her former life as a mermaid.

Every year on August 23, Copenhagen commemorates the Little Mermaid's birthday with a promenade down Langelinie. Celebrants dress up in mermaid costumes and formation swimmers entertain crowds by performing in the water near the statue. In 2010, for the first time since being installed in the city's harbor, the Little Mermaid statue left Copenhagen and traveled to Shanghai, where 70 million people viewed her.

MUTILATING THE MERMAID

Not everyone loves the Little Mermaid, however. In April 1964, vandals decapitated her—but she survived the beheading and was restored to her original state in time for summer vacationers to enjoy her. In 1984 two men cut off her arm and in 1998 she lost her head again—fortunately, her missing parts were returned and reattached. She's also been doused with paint, clothed in a burqa, and blasted off her perch.

Friendly Scandinavian Merfolk

nlike many merfolk, the Havman usually behaves in a kindly manner toward humans and sometimes willingly helps them. And unlike mermen in other parts of the world, this friendly fellow is generally described as being quite handsome as well—if you like blue skin, a green beard and hair, and the tail of a fish.

Havfrue, the Havman's feminine counterpart, is said to be beautiful with long, blonde hair that seafarers say she grooms with a golden comb. It's said that the Havfrue sometimes assumes human form and comes on land where she entices human males. Although both the Havman and Havfrue are generally considered benevolent, fishermen's legends warn that the female's appearance often presages storms or poor catches. They also claim that mariners who go out to sea and never return have been captured by mermaids—and maybe it's true.

Among their many mystical abilities, these merfolk reportedly possess the ability to see into the future. Scandinavian lore holds that a clairvoyant Havfrue predicted the birth of King Christian IV of Denmark and Norway in 1577.

Another male Scandinavian water spirit known as Fosse-Grim or Fossegrim is not only handsome but talented, too. Folklore says he plays a mean violin and his enchanting songs lure women and children into lakes or waterfalls, where they drown. But he may not intend to harm the people he attracts. Some stories describe romantic relationships between these mermen and human women, but in most instances Fosse-Grim eventually returns to his aquatic home.

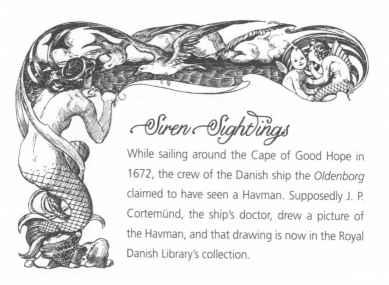

Siren Sightings

While sailing around the Cape of Good Hope in 1672, the crew of the Danish ship the *Oldenborg* claimed to have seen a Havman. Supposedly J. P. Cortemünd, the ship's doctor, drew a picture of the Havman, and that drawing is now in the Royal Danish Library's collection.

WHY ARE SWEDISH WATER LILIES RED?

A rare, wild red water lily named *Nymphaea alba var. rubra* grows only in parts of Sweden, including Lake Fagertärn. Folklore says the lily owes its origins to a girl who refused to marry a merman. When the merman tried to take her to his watery home, the girl stabbed herself instead and toppled into the lake. Her blood turned the water lilies red.

MINIATURE MERMEN

Usually we think of mermaids and mermen as being about the same size as human beings. But according to Kerry Colburn's *Mermaids*, "Norwegian fishermen hope to catch a marmel, a thumb-sized merman that brings good luck."

The Nixes

 n the rivers, lakes, and waterfalls of Germany and Poland live shapeshifting spirits known as nixes. They look completely human when seen on land, but nixes have a special quality humans don't—they can breathe and exist underwater. Both males and females can adopt human forms and come on land when it pleases them. Like other water spirits, nixes sometimes marry human beings and produce hybrid children. And like merfolk in other cultures, these mythical beings use their melodious voices to entice people. Some sources say the male nix can appear in many different shapes—including animals and even inanimate objects—while in the water, whereas the female always displays the typical mermaid's fishtail.

Nixes aren't usually as nice as the Scandinavian spirits; these water-men and their female partners entice human beings into their aquatic domains and drown them. You'll know that a person has been drowned by a nix if you see blue spots speckling the victim's recovered body.

How do you know if you're in the company of a nix? Legend says you can recognize a male nix by his red cap and a female by her red stockings. If you look closely, you'll also notice telltale dampness along the edges of his jacket and the hem of her skirt.

MERFOLK'S COMMON ORIGINS

Why do merfolk from different countries seem so much alike? Researchers, anthropologists, and linguists suggest that the reason so many similarities exist in legends about mermaids is that they're all rooted in early, pre-Christian conceptions of fertility goddesses. In virtually every part of the world, ancient people believed that deities ruled the rivers, lakes, and oceans. Such is the case with Scandinavian, German, and Polish merfolk. For example, the handsome freshwater spirit Fosse-Grim is also called näck, näkki, nøkk, and nøkken in Scandinavia and displays some of the same characteristics as the German nix (a.k.a. nixie, nixe, or nyx). The *Oxford English Dictionary* says "nix" derives from the Old High German word *Nichus*. Old Norse tales also refer to a mythical river- or brook-horse as a *nykr*, which may have been a predecessor of the merfolk.

THE TRICKY NIXIE

In the mid-nineteenth century, the Brothers Grimm wrote a fairy tale titled "The Nixie in the Pond" in which a female nixie promises a miller good fortune in exchange for his newborn son. When the boy grows up and becomes a man, the nixie captures him and drags him into her pond. But the man's wife tricks the nixie by leaving her gifts and eventually manages to free her husband from the pond.

Lorelei, the Rhine River Spirit

s German folklore tells us, once upon a time, a beautiful young woman named Lorelei was abandoned by her lover. But the other men in the town where she lived couldn't resist her and her charms caused a scandal. To solve the problem, the bishop sentenced her to be locked away in a convent for life. But on the way to her imprisonment, Lorelei asked the guards accompanying her to let her see her beloved Rhine River one last time. The distraught woman climbed to a high cliff overlooking the river and threw herself into the water—where she transformed into a nixie.

Supposedly Lorelei now inhabits a rock named for her, in the narrows of the Rhine near Sankt Goarshausen, Germany. An echo produced by the rock is said to be the sound of her singing. Today, tour boats ferry visitors safely to see the spot where the Rhine mermaid's enticing voice and great beauty once lured boatmen to their deaths.

River maids also play starring roles in Germanic music, art, and literature. Richard Wagner's famous nineteenth-century opera *Der Ring des Nibelungen* features three Rhine maidens, Wellgunde, Woglinde, and Flosshilde, who guard an underwater treasure known as the Rheingold. The opera is loosely based on the medieval epic poem, "Nibelungenlied" or "Song of the Nibelungs."

LORELEI COMES TO HOLLYWOOD

The Rhine River mermaid made an appearance in Hollywood in 1953, in the movie *Gentlemen Prefer Blondes*, based on Anita Loos's 1925 novel. The film starred Marilyn Monroe as Lorelei Lee, a beautiful blonde gold-digger with more than a touch of the seductive siren in her. And remember Superman's mysterious girlfriend, before Lois Lane came on the scene? This wheelchair-bound beauty named Lori Lemaris covered up her mermaid's tail with a blanket to hide her secret from the clueless Clark Kent.

The Warsaw Maiden

 nlike the dangerous and destructive mermaids said to inhabit waters elsewhere in the world, the mermaid of Warsaw, Poland, serves as the city's protector and benefactor. Warsaw's residents love their mermaid so much they made her the city's symbol in the seventeenth century. Her bronze statue graces the Old Town Market Square and she decorates Warsaw's coat of arms, holding a sword and a shield. The mermaid also shows up in art and architecture—including the door of St. John's Cathedral—and in the logos of numerous businesses in Poland's capital city.

The Warsaw Mermaid or "Warszawska Syrenka," sculpted by Konstanty Hegel, began watching over the city in the mid-nineteenth century. But she mysteriously disappeared during World War II—perhaps seeking a more peaceful place to live, as mermaids are known to do. In 2000, she resurfaced—supposedly discovered in a scrap yard—and once again took her place atop a stone pedestal in the town square. The pool beneath her shows her watery origins.

Various legends surround the mermaid and her connection to the city of Warsaw. One says the mermaid led a man named Wars to the spot on the river where he founded the city. In another tale a mermaid named Sawa from the Baltic Sea swam from Gdansk into the Vistula River and stopped to rest in Warsaw. She liked it so much she decided to stay. A merchant trapped her and held her prisoner, until a young fisherman named Wars heard her crying and helped her escape. In gratitude, she promised to aid fishermen and protect the town forevermore. The city's name comes from the merger of Wars and Sawa.

H.C.

The French Sirene Melusina

uring the Middle Ages, a water spirit called Melusina became the darling of the French aristocracy. Her story, however, is hardly a happy one. It begins when Raymond, the son of a bankrupt count, is adopted by a nobleman named Emmerick who becomes his friend. In a hunting incident, Raymond accidentally kills Emmerick and wanders about in grief until he comes upon a fountain deep in the forest. There he meets three mysterious women, including one named Melusina with whom he falls in love. He asks her to marry him and she agrees, with one condition: He must never see her on Saturday.

After the couple wed Melusina gives birth to several deformed children. One Saturday night, the curious Raymond spies on his wife in her bath—and sees that she has the tail of a snake. He blames her for defiling his family line and she leaves him because he broke his vow. According to legend, Melusina now flies about France heralding death and crying out when a tragedy is about to occur.

MELUSINA'S BIOGRAPHY

French historian Jean d'Arras compiled a work titled *Chronique de Melusine* in the fifteenth century, which chronicles the history of the Melusina myth. It remains the oldest book in existence on the subject.

MER MEANS SEA

Mer, the term we use for the merfolk species, comes from the French word for sea. Interestingly, the French word for mermaid is *sirene* and the word for merman is *triton*.

Italy's Sirena

> *"Supremely beautiful, forever combing her hair, just beyond reach of men, mermaids have beckoned the adventurous to the unknown and the promise of forbidden fruits."*

— Beatrice Phillpotts, *Mermaids*

 uring his return voyage from the New World in January 1493, Italian explorer Christopher Columbus claimed to have spotted three mermaids swimming in the waters near Haiti. Most likely Columbus saw manatees—he just thought he'd sighted mermaids because he, like other mariners of his time, believed all sorts of fantastic creatures inhabited the oceans of the world. That's because many early adventurers, including Columbus and Marco Polo, had read and drawn ideas from a popular fifteenth-century book titled *Imago Mundi*. Written by Cardinal Pierre d'Ailly, the book described a host of peculiar creatures including merfolk who supposedly lived in then-unknown parts of the globe.

Medieval manuscripts and Latin encyclopedias, such as *De Proprietatibus Rerum* by Bartholomeus Anglicus, described mermaids in detail. Christian authors warned seafarers that the lovely hybrid creatures were dangerous whores who seduced men, then killed and ate them. Merfolk provided appealing subjects for artists as well. The seductive *sirena* (the Italian word for mermaid) adorned the pages of many illuminated manuscripts and illustrated books from the medieval and Renaissance periods.

One of the most intriguing examples of mermaid sculpture dominates the Piazza Nettuno in Bologna, Italy. This erotic fountain features double-tailed mermaids suggestively spreading their tails while enticingly squeezing water from their shapely breasts. Commissioned to celebrate Pope Pius IV's election in 1559 and sculpted by artist Giambologna, the bronze Fontana di Nettuno—which also depicts Neptune in all his naked glory—raised a good deal of controversy when it was unveiled. But the Pope gave the fountain his blessing, saying, "For Bologna it is alright."

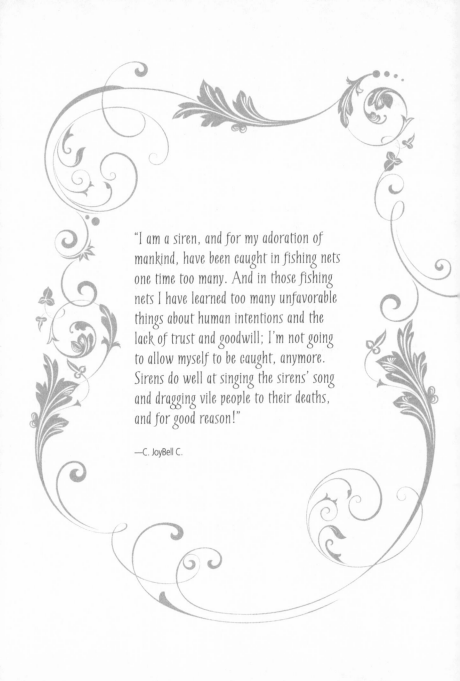

"I am a siren, and for my adoration of mankind, have been caught in fishing nets one time too many. And in those fishing nets I have learned too many unfavorable things about human intentions and the lack of trust and goodwill; I'm not going to allow myself to be caught, anymore. Sirens do well at singing the sirens' song and dragging vile people to their deaths, and for good reason!"

—C. JoyBell C.

CHAPTER 7

Russian Rusalky AND OTHER Slavic Merfolk

IN THE LORE and legends of Russia, the Ukraine, the Baltic regions, and parts of Eastern Europe one of the most prevalent water spirits is the rusalka (plural rusalky or rusalki). Usually, the rusalka appears as a dangerous or demonic creature—even as a succubus. Unlike mermaids in other parts of the world, the rusalka boasts a unique characteristic: She loves to dance.

The Russian Rusalky

ussian rusalky are always female—males of the species don't seem to exist. Accounts of what a rusalka looks like, however, vary from region to region. It depends on whom you ask and where the storyteller lives. Some tales describe rusalky as fish-woman hybrids, akin to the mermaids who populate folklore in other parts of the world. But in Siberia, rusalky reportedly look more like yetis than lovely mermaids. Parallels also exist between these Russian spirits and the German nixes—both river creatures are malevolent tricksters who come on land and nab unwitting humans. A Russian proverb warns, "Not everything is a mermaid that dives into the water."

Typically freshwater beings, they usually live at the bottoms of rivers. At night they leave their watery abodes and shapeshift into two-legged humanoids who make their way along the riverbanks and fields. There they sing and dance enticingly in order to enchant men whom they find attractive—then they lure their captives back to the river and drown them.

Like other mermaids, rusalky can be spotted sitting near the lakes or rivers where they live, combing their long hair. At night they sometimes shed their fishtails and climb trees or swing from the branches, singing more sweetly than songbirds.

The great Czech composer Antonin Dvorak wrote an opera titled *Rusalka*, which premiered in Prague in 1901 and has endured as his most successful opera. With lyrics by poet and librettist Jaroslav Kvapil, *Rusalka* tells a Slavic version of Friedrich de la Motte Fouqué's *Undine* and Hans Christian Andersen's "The Little Mermaid."

MODERN MERMAIDS

Two Russian "mermaids," Semenova Veronika and Stikhilyas Valeriya, perform graceful, underwater acrobatics for audiences around the world. These young women are synchronized swimmers who trained for five years to learn their craft, which requires them to hold their breath for up to several minutes at a time. If you can't see the real thing, you can watch their aquatic skills on *www.mid-day.com* as they cavort in the aquarium at Mumbai's Ocean restaurant.

Restless Ghosts

ther legends describe the rusalky as female ghosts who haunt lakes and waterways. These legends explain that the rusalky represent the souls of young women who died in or near bodies of water. In many cases, the women died violently, as murder victims or suicides. Because they died prematurely and unnaturally, they continue to be bound to Earth as spirits for the length of what would have been their normal lives. Only if a murdered ghost's death is avenged can her spirit finally rest.

Still other tales say rusalky are the souls of unbaptized babies. Some of these disembodied spirits were babies born out of wedlock and drowned by their mothers. Folklore says they roam the land, searching for someone to baptize them so they can finally find peace. According to some accounts, ghostly rusalky can be violent, though others insist they're not usually malicious if you leave them alone.

A ten-minute-long Russian movie titled *Rusalka* received an Oscar nomination for Best Short Animated Film. Directed by Aleksandr Petrov in 1996, it used a special paint-on-glass technique. In the story, a young monk discovers a beautiful naked woman in a river and falls in love with her. The woman turns out to be a rusalka, the spirit of a girl the young monk's master rejected many years ago. As is typical in much Russian folklore, the rusalka seeks vengeance on the man who treated her badly.

A RUSALKA VAMPIRE?

The first book in C. J. Cherryh's fantasy trilogy, *The Russian Stories*, features a rusalka named Eveshka. Published in 1989, *Rusalka* takes place in pre-Christian Russia and tells the story of a wizard's murdered daughter who becomes a ghost. The rusalka exists by sucking the vitality out of other living things.

Ukrainian Rusalky

 ccording to the *Encyclopedia of Ukraine*, Ukranian rusalky are water nymphs who resemble pretty, naked young females with long green or blonde hair upon which they wear wreaths woven from marsh plants. Some accounts say their "eyes blaze like green fire" and their white skin seems almost translucent. However, these shapeshifters possess the ability to transform themselves into animals or anthropomorphic creatures when it pleases them.

These souls of drowned girls and unbaptized children live in underwater crystal cities most of the year, but emerge in the spring on Rusalka Easter (about seven to eight weeks after Christian Easter) when they dance and play on land. During Rusalka Week or Green Week, which usually occurs in early June, the rusalky reportedly reach their most dangerous peak. Superstitious people avoid swimming at this time for fear of being pulled underwater by the treacherous water nymphs.

While on land the rusalky appear as lighthearted young girls, but despite their winsomeness they can be dangerous to humans. Folktales say they attract bachelors by singing, and then either drown or tickle their victims to death. Sometimes a rusalka's laugh is enough to kill a man. To protect themselves against the wicked wiles of the rusalky, Ukrainian men wear wormwood or lovage as amulets, or carry pieces of lucky cloth.

RUSALKA DANCING:
A FERTILITY RITE

The rusalka's dancing supposedly aids the growth of grain—giving her a link with the fertility deities of other cultures.

Siren Sightings

On June 15, 1608, English seafarer and explorer Henry Hudson was searching the Arctic Circle near Russia for a new route to the East Indies when a crewman spotted a mermaid. Hudson recorded in his log that at 75° 7' N "one of our companie looking overboard saw a mermaid, and calling up some of the companie to see her, one more came up, and by that time she was close to the ship's side, looking earnestly upon the men: a little after, a Sea came and overturned her: From the Navill upward, her backe and breasts were like a woman's . . . her body as big as one of us; her skin very white; and long haire hanging down behinde, of colour blacke; in her going down they saw her tayle, which was like the tayle of a Porposse, and speckled like a Macrell. Their names that saw her were Thomas Hilles and Robert Rayner."

THEY WALK AMONG US

How can you spot a rusalka? First, her eyes have no pupils, giving her a rather demented look. Second, her hair is always wet, and if it dries she'll die. Consequently, she can't survive long on land. Her comb, however, serves as a talisman, for with it she can magically make water appear if she gets stranded.

Slavic Water Spirits

 lthough the rusalky dominate Russian and Slavic merfolk myths, a few old legends speak about other types of water spirits. These beings bear similarities to those found in the folklore of other cultures, including the Greek water nymphs and the Indian snake deities.

Some Slavic legends mention mermen who marry rusalky. Like the females, they may be the ghosts of people who died unnatural deaths. These male water spirits, called wodjanoj or vodianoi, are said to be shapeshifters and can transform themselves into fish. These couples, folklore says, live in underwater castles built from parts of sunken ships. Unlike their beautiful mates, the ugly males sport long green beards and have bodies covered with scales and slime. The mermen can be vindictive—they may drown humans who offend them or capture people and keep them in the aquatic realm as slaves.

Slavic lore also includes stories of human-snake hybrids with magical powers. In one folktale a water snake comes ashore and tricks a girl into marrying him. The couple lives in his home at the bottom of a pond, where the snake transforms into a human-looking being, and they have two children together.

After three years, the wife decides to visit her mother on land. She tells her mother about her shapeshifting husband and her underwater life. But the mother, not wanting to lose her daughter, tricks the snake-man and chops off his head. The brokenhearted wife then changes herself and her children into birds.

Siren Sightings

In February 2007, a strange aquatic creature was supposedly captured in the Sea of Azov by villagers from Russia's Rostov region. The fishermen, initially believing they'd caught an alien or a mermaid, took pictures of it with a cell phone. The strange whitish creature resembled a shark and weighed about 220 pounds. Andrei Gorodovoi, chairman of the Anomalous Phenomena Service, called it "an anomalous being" and specialists said they'd never seen anything like it. Unfortunately, scientists can't study the rare creature, because after filming it the fishermen ate it and pronounced it delicious.

The Iele

 omanian mythology speaks of the Iele, female spirits similar to the rusalky who make their homes in ponds, marshes, and springs. These magical beings can be seen dancing on land at night with their long hair flowing, holding candles and wearing nothing but bells around their ankles. Often they seem as translucent as ghosts, but they sometimes inhabit the shapely bodies of beautiful young women. Their mesmerizing dancing and enchanting singing captivate humans.

The Iele can be temperamental and may cause people who displease them to fall asleep for long periods of time—or to disappear altogether. Other stories say a human who hears them singing instantly turns mute. The ground on which they dance looks scorched afterward and nothing but mushrooms will grow there from then on.

Some Romanians call the Iele "the devil's daughters." Woe be to someone who angers the Iele, for these malicious spirits take revenge by possessing the person. In this demonic state, known as *Luat din Calus*, the deranged individual may suffer all sorts of horrible consequences including loss of sight and/or hearing. Some injure themselves or others—they may even commit murder. The only people who supposedly can remove the Iele's curse are the Calusari, a group of healers with magical powers who perform a ritual dance to cure victims.

Not all Iele fall into the category of water spirits, however. Legends depict them as nature fairies of various kinds, some of whom live in caves, forests, and mountains, or fly about in the sky.

"I am the star that rises from the sea, the
      twilight sea
I bring men dreams that rule their destiny.
I bring the dream-tides to the souls of men;
The tides that ebb and flow and ebb again—
These are my secrets, these belong to me."

—Dion Fortune

CHAPTER 8

African AND Indian Mermaids

MANY OF THE WORLD'S most ancient mermaid myths come from Africa, India, and the Middle East—the earliest centers of civilization. People in these parts of the world told tales of curious aquatic beings and powerful water deities long before Europe and the Americas were settled. Their stories, handed down through countless generations, influenced conceptions of mermaids, sea gods and goddesses, and other water deities up until the present time.

Mami Wata

"Mami Wata as the Divine African Mother/God/dess has been worshiped and celebrated around the world for thousands of years. From Egypt as *Isis,* in Asia Minor (Ephesus) as *Sibyl (Cyeble),* in Greece as *Rhea, Hekate* and *Artemis,* and in Rome as the great *Magna Mater* amongst her other holy names."

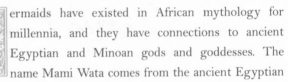

—Mama Zogbé, "Mami Wata: From Myth to Divine Reality"

ermaids have existed in African mythology for millennia, and they have connections to ancient Egyptian and Minoan gods and goddesses. The name Mami Wata comes from the ancient Egyptian and Ethiopian word *mama* meaning "truth, wisdom" and *uat-ur* meaning "ocean water." In some early languages of the Sudan, *wata* means "woman." Other sources, mostly in the West, suggest Mami Wata is pidgin English for "Mother Water," though this is unlikely considering that the deities existed in African culture and folklore long before the English language infiltrated that continent.

Although commonly thought to be a single deity, "Mami Wata" actually refers to a pantheon of African water deities; these deities are part of Africa's ancient spiritual belief system, which was matriarchal like those in many other areas throughout the world prior to the ascent of the patriarchal religious structures typically embraced today. Early depictions of Mami Wata show them with the heads and torsos of humans and the lower bodies of either fish or snakes—much like mermaids in other parts of the world. These water spirits can be either masculine or feminine, but are usually thought of as feminine. In later representations, Mami Wata morphed into a singular image of a voluptuous, long-haired black woman with a large snake—symbol of wisdom and spiritual power—wrapped around her body.

Like their mermaid counterparts elsewhere, Mami Wata enjoy their fancy combs, mirrors, and jewelry. To solicit their aid, a supplicant might make an offering of these gifts—Mami Wata love bling!

GODDESS OR SNAKE CHARMER?

Der Schlagenbandinger, an Art Nouveau chromolithograph of a beautiful Hamburg snake charmer created by German artist Felix Schlesinger, contributed to our contemporary conception of Mami Wata. Western images sometimes present Mami Wata as a seductive love goddess or sensual female shapeshifter who can take the form of a mermaid, snake priestess, or human woman. The name Mami Wata may even be used as a slang term for a beautiful woman.

Benevolent Beauties

nlike the mischievous, tempestuous, or downright destructive merfolk who turn up in the myths of other parts of the world, Mami Wata are generally viewed as benevolent and powerful divinities who govern natural cycles, including the Nile's overflow, agriculture, fishing, hunting, and so on. They're said to assist human beings physically and spiritually, and to provide food, shelter, protection, healing, and all the other necessities for life on Earth. Therefore, legends sometimes link these spirits with wealth and abundance—they bring prosperity to humans. As fertility goddesses, they watch over mothers and children. Some sources also credit them with guiding seers, mystics, and healers.

Mami Wata sometimes capture swimmers or sailors and shepherd them into other worlds—either the underwater realm or the spirit plane (which may be the same thing, given that water in mythology often symbolizes intuition and spirituality). If these human abductees return to land, they display a greater spiritual awareness and often prosper as a result of their experiences with Mami Wata. They may even come back with psychic ability or other extraordinary skills.

But some sources warn that Mami Wata aren't always gentle and generous—they can also be capricious and cantankerous. If a person disobeys them, they may drown the errant follower or thrust him into a world of confusion, delirium, and disease.

KEEPING THE SPIRIT ALIVE

The Mami Wata Healers Society of North America, Inc., is a nonprofit "ancestral, Afro-religious organization committed to the resurrection, establishment, dissemination and maintenance of the Mami Wata and Yeveh Vodoun spiritual and ritual traditions, brought to the North American shores by enslaved Africans." (See *www.mamiwata.com* for more information.)

Yemaya

"Yemaya reminds us that even the worst catastrophes can be endured and that, with her help, we can learn to negotiate the ebbs and flows of change in our lives with her wisdom, courage, and grace."

—Sharon Turnbull, author of *Goddess Gift*

 emaya, or Yemoja, goddess of the ocean, abides at the heart of several African religions. Her full name, Yey Omo Eja, means "mother whose children are the fish." Often depicted as a mermaid, this mother goddess of the Yoruba religion originally ruled the Ogun River, the largest and most powerful waterway in Nigeria. When Africans were brought to the New World, Yemaya came with them and watched over them as they endured the arduous voyage and travails of slavery.

As her African worshipers experienced the sea for the first time, Yemaya's powers expanded and she gained dominion over the ocean as well. But she only represents the upper portion of the ocean, the part that contains most of the sea life, the source of nourishment— for this mother deity generously provides for her human children. You could even think of the ebb and flow of the ocean's tides as a great cradle in which the goddess Yemaya rocks us all.

Like most water deities and mermaids, Yemaya exudes a potent sexuality. Usually she is portrayed as voluptuous, with large breasts, hips, and buttocks that suggest her fertility. The rolling tides symbolize the motion of her undulating walk. She wears seven blue-and-white skirts, which signify the seven seas.

Despite her caring, comforting, and compassionate nature, Yemaya can be temperamental—just like the ocean. Provoke her at your peril, for this protective goddess drowns those who harm her children.

YEMAYA'S GIFT TO HUMANITY

Yemaya's energy flows through seashells, and folklore says she gave shells to human beings so they could listen to her voice. Hold a shell to your ear—can you hear Yemaya speaking to you?

PETITIONING YEMAYA

How can you win Yemaya's favor and protection? Honor her with gifts of flowers, jewelry, oranges, and pound cake. Like many water deities (and women), she also loves perfume.

Oshun

"I am the honey-sweet voice of the waters. I am the flowing of a woman's skirts as she dances her life."

—Thalia Took, creator of *The Goddess Oracle Deck*

aughter of the sea goddess Yemaya, Oshun (or Ochun) abides in freshwater and is sometimes known as the goddess of luxury and love. Like many water deities, she represents fertility, prosperity, nourishment, and healing. And, like other African goddesses, this beloved deity protects her people and provides for them.

Some images of Oshun show her as a typical mermaid, with the torso of a beautiful woman and the tail of a fish. Others depict her as a lovely and charismatic young human female. In addition to the usual mirror and comb, Oshun sometimes holds a golden fan. This luxury-loving lady adores jewelry, and artists often picture her decked out in gems.

Although Oshun can be considered vain and more than a little self-indulgent, she's one of the best-natured of all the water deities. This benevolent river goddess lacks the dark and dangerous qualities often associated with mermaids in other cultures. Generous, kind-hearted, and compassionate, she likes to shower her adoring followers with gifts and wants everyone to be happy. The only time she gets angry is when someone harms children, for Oshun serves as their protectress.

LOVE-CASTING

Legend says Oshun possesses the gifts of divination and spell-casting. Being a love goddess, she particularly enjoys casting love spells. But before you ask her for magical help, remember the old saying: Be careful what you wish for!

Desperately Seeking Oshun

here can you find this generous and lusty lady? First try the Ogun River in Nigeria. But if you can't make it to Africa, legend says she resides in streams, rivers, and lakes everywhere. Some sources say this sensuous goddess revels in beauty and likes to hang out in all the luxurious places human women frequent: spas, jewelry stores, boutiques, and beauty shops. That sexy bottle-blonde getting a seaweed wrap at your favorite day spa might just be Oshun!

If you're serious about making contact with Oshun, one way to get her attention is to present her with a gift. Deities are accustomed to receiving offerings from people who seek their aid—and Oshun is no exception. She'll be glad to assist you in the game of love, but first it's a good idea to give this notoriously decadent mermaid-goddess a few goodies. She adores gold and amber jewelry (but she'll settle for brass if gold is out of your price range). She's a big fan of perfume, too, particularly lush, sensual fragrances like amber, patchouli, and frankincense. Sweet foods of all kinds delight her, too, especially honey. Often artists depict her with a honeypot dangling from her hips—innuendo intended! Cinnamon, yams, and pumpkins also tempt her taste buds. And, like most females, Oshun adores flowers—yellow roses most of all.

Set up an altar dedicated to her. Place the offerings on it and sing to her or play African music. Pretty soon you'll sense her presence. Ask her to help you—most likely, she'll agree.

Africa's River Spirits

"In the sea of Angola mermaids are frequently caught which resemble the human species. They are taken in nets, and killed . . . and are heard to shriek and cry like women."

—Henry Lee, *Sea Fables Explained*

ore than 4,100 miles from its source to its end, the mighty Nile is the longest river in the world. The Congo River, at nearly 3,000 miles, flows through Africa's center and ranks eighth. Is it any surprise, then, that African mythology contains lots of river deities? Mami Wata and Oshun may be the best-known and most-beloved river goddesses in African folklore, but they aren't the only ones.

African legends frequently mention hybrid water creatures who live in the rivers and lakes—and who may have inspired our modern-day conceptions of mermaids. Among these mysterious beings we find snakelike spirits and merfolk with mystical powers. The legends of Lamba in south-central Africa speak of a shapeshifting, fishtailed river snake known as a *funkwe* who, like merfolk in other cultures, can transform himself into a two-legged being and come on land to snare a human wife. The deadly *chitapo* of the Congo might drag an unsuspecting human underwater and drown him, or kill him simply with a look—you don't want to get up close and personal with her! Even if these deities don't destroy a man, they can disrupt his domestic harmony and happiness, for their seductive wiles are said to be irresistible.

But snakes also represent healing, fertility, and transformation—and the chitapo supposedly help barren women conceive. The water spirits of Cameroon, known as Jengu, are believed to cure diseases and often serve as messengers between the world of humans and that of spirits.

THE MYSTERIOUS CHITAPO

The dangerous and mysterious chitapo, said to live in Lake Kashiba and other African bodies of water, lures people by floating baskets, sleeping mats, and various household objects on the water's surface. Anthropologist Brian Siegel, PhD, of Furman University's religion department explains that local legends warn against drinking or eating fish from bodies of water where the chitapo dwells. Sometimes described as a "shadowy apparition," the evil water spirit is reputed to have swallowed up numerous men, women, and children who got too close to the haunted waters.

Mamba Muntu: A Modern Mermaid

frica, with its many rich and diverse cultures, is home to myriad mermaids—these lovely creatures occupy both the rivers and the oceans of this vast continent. But Professor Brian Siegel of Furman University contends that the mermaid image we know today didn't come about until the twentieth century and is really a combination of early African water spirits and European legends.

Among these blended beauties we find the mermaid Mamba Muntu, or "Snake Woman," whose picture graces taverns in various parts of Africa. As we might expect, she is exquisitely beautiful and seductive, and like Oshun, she frequently shows up arrayed with plenty of jewelry—including a watch, which suggests a recent Western influence, for early water deities didn't have to worry about being on time. Around her lush body Mamba Muntu wears a large snake, à la Mami Wata. But unlike Mami Wata and the water goddesses Yemaya and Oshun, this hybrid female often appears with the light skin and blonde hair of northern European women, rather than the dark and sultry features of African deities.

She's not as kind, generous, and compassionate as the native goddesses either—perhaps another sign of Western infiltration into the indigenous culture. Mamba Muntu, like many of her merfolk kin, can be destructive and may torment or kill human beings without warning. But if a man manages to steal her precious comb, he can use it for personal gain, specifically for wealth and power.

India's Nagas and Naginis

"[Nagini's] mission is threefold: to bestow wisdom on those who are worthy, to prevent access to sacred knowledge to those not deserving, and to prevent sacred teachings from being lost."

—Nancy Blair, *Goddesses for Every Season*

 or millennia, Hindu and Buddhist mythology has had a love-hate relationship with the enigmatic snake-people known as the nagas (males) and naginis (females). These mythical beings are usually considered to be semidivine in nature, half-human and half-serpent—but like most merfolk they can appear with completely human or completely snaky bodies. Females, especially, are said to be stunningly beautiful.

Considered nature spirits in Vedic tradition, they live at the bottom of lakes, rivers, and streams in magnificent palaces where they guard their treasure. Legends credit them with performing many roles, from protecting the waters of the world to guarding sacred knowledge. Like many water deities, they're both creators and destroyers. They bring rain, but also cause floods. However, some sources say they only show their destructive sides in retaliation for humankind's mistreatment of nature and the environment.

The nagas and naginis play a key role in the ancient Hindu epic *Mahabharata*, where they tend to get a bad rap for being cruel predators who persecute other creatures. But legends also associate these aquatic divinities with hidden knowledge, transformation, and immortality. And, like many water deities and serpents, they're potent fertility symbols.

Artists frequently depict nagas and naginis with human torsos and snaky lower bodies, or with multiple snakeheads—often seven, but sometimes as many as a thousand. But these shapeshifters can change themselves into human beings if they choose. Not limited to India, nagas and naginis appear in the lore and legends of other Asian nations, where they assume various forms.

Notable Nagas and Naginis

 anasa, the goddess of snakes, is considered the daughter of the great Hindu god Shiva. This prominent and revered nagini represents fertility and prosperity. Her powers include the ability to cure snakebites and neutralize poisons—she saved Shiva's life after he unknowingly drank poison.

Vasuki, Manasa's brother, is one of the naga kings. Legend says he wears a great gem on his head. In Buddhist mythology, he leads the nagas who protect the Buddha. In Hindu lore, he protects Vishnu.

The naga lord Varuna is in charge of the weather—his powers include the ability to bring life-giving rain and to raise storms. Some myths credit him as the ruler of the ocean and rivers, even as the king of the cosmos. When someone drowned, the person's soul went to Varuna.

Kanya, the nagini of the three realms, protects underwater treasures and spiritual ones as well. Sometimes depicted with a jewel in her forehead and wings on her shoulders, she holds a shell from which she pours the waters of wisdom onto humanity.

King of all the nagas, Sesha is considered a creator god. In his cobra-like hood he holds the planets. He often appears aboard an arching, wave-like raft that floats upon the cosmic ocean. Legend says he stabilized the world at the Buddha's request and still supports the Earth today. In the *Mahabharata*, Brahma entrusts Sesha with the great responsibility of holding the world on his head.

BRAHMA'S ORDERS

Legend says Brahma forced the nagas and naginis off the face of the Earth and into the "nether regions" because they were overpopulating the world. He also ordered them to bite only evil people.

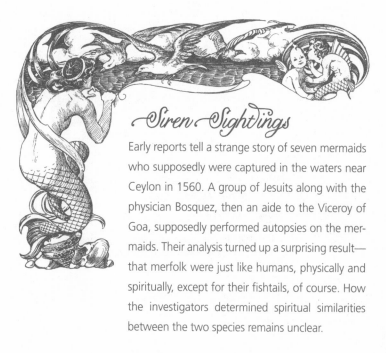

Siren Sightings

Early reports tell a strange story of seven mermaids who supposedly were captured in the waters near Ceylon in 1560. A group of Jesuits along with the physician Bosquez, then an aide to the Viceroy of Goa, supposedly performed autopsies on the mermaids. Their analysis turned up a surprising result— that merfolk were just like humans, physically and spiritually, except for their fishtails, of course. How the investigators determined spiritual similarities between the two species remains unclear.

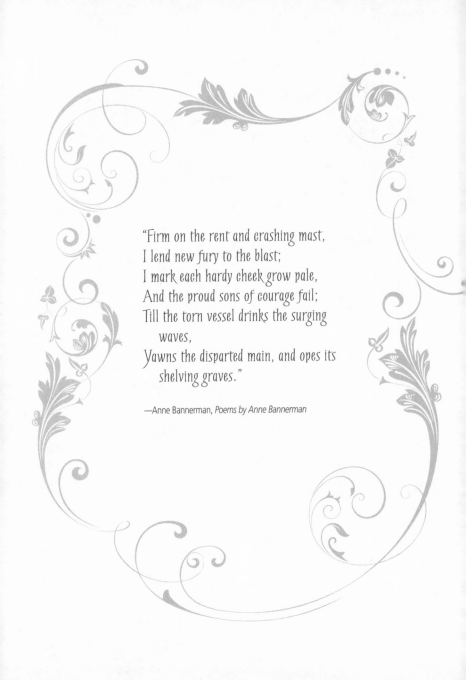

"Firm on the rent and crashing mast,
I lend new fury to the blast;
I mark each hardy cheek grow pale,
And the proud sons of courage fail;
Till the torn vessel drinks the surging
      waves,
Yawns the disparted main, and opes its
      shelving graves."

—Anne Bannerman, *Poems by Anne Bannerman*

CHAPTER 9

Mermaids OF THE Far East

ELEGANT, WISE, AND GIFTED in music and the arts, mermaids of the Far East have it all. The dazzling beauties who live in Asia's oceans, lakes, and rivers bring good fortune to human-kind. Some propel themselves through the waters with the tails of fish or snakes—like mermaids in other parts of the world. But the lovely aquatic ladies of China and Japan often ally themselves with another mythical being—the dragon. Whether they ride dragons or shapeshift into these magical creatures, Asian water divinities possess strength, majesty, and creative power worthy of reverence and awe.

Benton the Beautiful

ong, long ago Benton, a.k.a. Benzaiten, enriched the world with her beauty, talent, and wisdom. Inspired by Saraswati, the Hindu goddess of water, poetry, music, and knowledge, Benton came to Japan along with Buddhism in the sixth century. Originally a water deity, she presided over Japan's geishas and served as their patroness, sharing her grace, knowledge, and artistic abilities with them. But over time, her popularity, status, and responsibilities grew and early in the seventeenth century the wealthy business and educated classes adopted her as a goddess of prosperity. She's the only female member of the prestigious Shinto pantheon the Seven Lucky Gods or Shichi Fukujin.

This gorgeous and beloved water goddess frequently shows up riding a dragon—sometimes a snake or sea serpent—while playing a lute. She can also transform herself into one of these reptilian creatures when she wants to. Myth says she came to Earth to stop an evil dragon from gobbling up children. As a result, she rose to the position of a protector-deity who guards her people and prevents natural disasters.

With so many jobs to do, it's a good thing Benton has lots of hands—artists show her with four, six, or even eight. In her hands she clasps a number of objects: a jewel (either a pearl or jade), a sword, a bow, an arrow, a wheel, a key, a long pestle, a silk rope. She also holds a *biwa*, a traditional Japanese mandolin or lute. Two of her hands are usually pressed together in prayer, signifying her devotion.

SHRINES AND STATUES

Shrines and temples to Benton dapple the Japanese country-side, often built near rivers, ponds, and other bodies of water. So beloved is she that myth says the island Enoshima in Sagami Bay, about 30 miles from Tokyo, emerged from the sea for the express purpose of enshrining her. Statues of her grace Japan's landscape, too; the three largest are in Enoshima, Chikubushima, and Inokashira. Tokyo's Inokashira Park includes a shrine and dragon-shaped statue of Benton, located in a pond where visitors can wash coins to attract good luck and prosperity.

The Lady of Luck and Love

t's easy to draw parallels between Benton, Venus, and Aphrodite. Mythology describes these deities as goddesses of love and the arts. They're also linked with luxury, good fortune, and happiness. And, because in so many countries water symbolizes fertility and abundance—even life itself—these divinities have water connections, too.

From the time she arrived in Japanese culture 1,500 years ago, Benton served as the patron of geishas, those gorgeous epitomes of beauty, grace, artistic ability, and love. But the geishas soon had to share their beloved goddess with other admirers—artists and musicians, writers and entertainers, restaurateurs and tavern keepers, gamblers and good luck seekers of all kinds. Believed to bring money and material gain to those who worshiped her, Benton became the darling of the elite classes, who gave her a place among the Seven Lucky Gods.

Lovers, too, petition Benton for blessings. Said to promote happiness in relationships, her aid is often sought by women who want to secure a fortunate marriage or resolve problems with a mate. Of course, this generous spirit always offers her help.

Naturally, you would expect a prosperity goddess to display her wealth and artists often depict Benton with heavenly jewels. Her jewels, though, aren't mere baubles—they possess magical powers. That special pearl or piece of jade she holds gives her the ability to grant wishes. Today, modern Japanese keep carved statues and idols of her in their homes and workplaces as good luck charms, hoping she'll bless them with riches.

THE POWER OF LOVE

Legend says Benton tamed an evil dragon that had been devouring children. To convince him to stop, Benton married the dragon, ostensibly transforming his bad qualities through the power of love. Images sometimes show Benton riding on a white dragon, snake, or sea serpent—symbols of jealousy. To avoid disharmony, men and women who seek happiness in a relationship visit her shrine separately rather than together.

A Mermaid on the Menu?

he Japanese diet contains lots of fish—including a strange "fish-woman" called a ningyo, according to some legends. This peculiar sea creature, which looks more like a cross between a monkey and a fish than a typical mermaid, sparkles with golden scales and utters a flute-like sound, though it can't actually speak. The ningyo's flesh, said to be aromatic and quite appetizing, is more than just tasty—it's magical. Eating it supposedly confers immortality on the diner.

An old story tells of a fisherman who caught an unusual fish with a face like that of a human being. When he served it to his guests at a party, they recoiled from its eerie appearance and refused to eat it. But one man who'd drunk too much sake took it home and fed it to his teenage daughter—who from then on never aged physically and lived to be 800 years old.

Despite its delectable flavor and promise of eternal youth, fishermen who catch it usually throw it back—the ningyo, it seems, brings bad luck. Often its appearance presages storms, and misfortunes or tragedies of all kinds may befall the person who catches it. If it washes up on land, the ningyo can be a harbinger of war or catastrophe.

FISH OR WATER FAIRY?

Some sources describe the ningyo as a type of water fairy, with a human face and the body of a fish, who lives in a beautiful castle at the bottom of the sea. This sensuous being wears silky, translucent garments that ripple like the ocean's waves about her body. Only rarely does she cry—when she does, her tears become pearls.

The Circus Mermaid

n 1842, Phineas T. Barnum of circus fame amazed curiosity seekers with a freakish display called the "Feejee (or Fiji) Mermaid." At his American Museum in New York City, Barnum exhibited what he claimed was a mummified specimen of a mermaid caught near the Fiji Islands in the South Seas.

But instead of getting to view a beautiful young fish-girl hybrid, as promised by Barnum's come-on, shocked visitors witnessed a bizarre creature that resembled the Japanese ningyo, with a monkey-like head and torso and a fishy lower body.

As it turned out, the Feejee Mermaid really was a monkey-fish composite. Apparently, Barnum had rented the monstrosity from a Boston museum owner. The Feejee Mermaid was only one of countless fakes fabricated in Asia since the sixteenth century. The fraudulent "mermaids" featured the actual head of a monkey and the body of a fish, neatly sewn together and dried to a withered, leather-like mummy. Barnum wasn't the first to try this scam. Decades earlier a sea captain named Samuel Barrett Eades exhibited a similar creature, but his hoax failed to capture the public's interest—perhaps because he lacked Barnum's notoriety and marketing skills.

The infamous Feejee Mermaid mysteriously turned up again in 1973. Since then, pictures and stories about similar creatures have appeared on various Internet sites—some even claimed the "mermaids" washed up on a beach in India after the 2004 tsunami.

Hoori, the Fisherman/Merman

nce upon a time, legend says two royal brothers named Hoderi, a great fisherman, and Hoori, a renowned hunter, lived in Japan. The older brother, Hoderi, loaned his lucky fishhook to Hoori to see if it would enable the younger brother to be a successful fisherman as well. But Hoori caught no fish—what's more, he lost Hoderi's favorite fishhook.

Hoderi insisted that Hoori find his fishhook, so the younger brother descended to the bottom of the sea to search for it. Once there, he met Toyotama (which means "rich jewel"), daughter of the sea god, and married her. They lived together happily in an underwater palace, but after three years Hoori began to miss Japan. The benevolent sea god gave him the long-lost fishhook, and Hoori went home to return it to his brother.

Toyotama, pregnant with the couple's son, asked her husband to build a house for her on land where she could give birth to the child and said she would join him when the time came. But first she exacted a promise from him: He would not attempt to see her during the birth. Hoori, though, couldn't resist the temptation and spied on his wife—and discovered she was truly a dragon. When she realized he'd broken his vow, she left Hoori and the child and returned to the sea god's castle under the sea. Toyotama's sister raised the baby, and when he grew up she married him. Mythology says one of their children became Japan's first emperor, Jimmu Tenno.

The Japanese Kappa

re the kappa frightful water demons that drag children underwater and devour them? Or supernatural beings that irrigate farmers' fields and help doctors set bones? Actually, a bit of both, according to Japanese folklore. Supposedly found in Japan's rivers and lakes, these odd creatures look like large monkeys—but instead of being covered with fur, they have fish scales or hard shells similar to those of turtles. Said to be yellowish-green in color, the kappa have webbed hands and feet, and reportedly smell like fish. But don't let the kappa's small stature fool you—these creatures are amazingly strong. They even come on land to attack horses, cattle, and other farm animals and drink their blood.

So how can you escape a kappa's deadly clutches? Take advantage of its most peculiar characteristic, a bowl-like indentation at the top of its head that contains water. If that water spills, the kappa loses its power. The creature is said to have a keen respect for good manners and will bow to you if you bow to it first—then its liquid life force flows out onto the ground and waters crops.

Here's another trick to use against a kappa: Appeal to its taste buds. Folktales say the kappa loves cucumbers, so if you intend to go near the water carry a few of these vegetables with you and toss them to the beast if it approaches. It may choose to eat the cucumbers instead of you!

THE KAPPA'S GIFT

Even monsters can have good qualities, and the kappa are credited with teaching humans how to set broken bones. Here's how folklore says it happened: A kappa, pretending to be human, tricked many people into playing a children's game that involved pulling the kappa's finger. When they did, he dragged them underwater and drowned them. Finally, a daring young man rode up to the kappa on horseback and when the creature grabbed his hand the man urged his horse forward. The galloping horse dragged the kappa until it promised to share its knowledge of healing bones with the rider. The man reined in his horse and the kappa told him the secret, which enabled the man to become a famous doctor.

Dragon Ladies

"When rain is to be expected, the dragons sing and their voices are like the sound made by striking copper basins. Their saliva can produce all kinds of perfume."

—Wang Fu, Chinese scholar (Han dynasty, 206 B.C.E. to C.E. 220)

e don't find much about mermaids in Chinese mythology. What we do find are female dragons whose magical qualities and dazzling beauty remind us of mermaids in other cultures. Most of these mythical creatures, each one covered with 117 sparkling fish scales, live in Asia's seas, lakes, and rivers—but they can change themselves into humans or fly in the air whenever they choose.

To the Chinese, dragons represent supreme power. These beloved mystical and spiritual entities bring prosperity, wisdom, and good luck of all kinds. Like water divinities around the world, China's dragons are potent nature spirits who not only rule the Eastern world's waterways, but also control the weather—particularly rain. Don't cross them or fail to show them proper respect for they can be vain, and—like mermaids elsewhere—have been known to whip up torrential storms and floods when humans displease them. Some dragons you should keep in mind are:

The four Dragon Kings rule the seas.

These dragons reside in underwater crystal castles, where crab generals and shrimp soldiers guard them and protect them from harm.

Panlong lives in freshwater.

Also called the Coiling Dragon, Panlong inhabits China's lakes and ponds.

Huanglong offers wisdom.

Known as the Yellow Dragon, Huanglong is credited with having taught writing to the Emperor Fu Shi.

Li makes its home in the ocean.

Sometimes called the Homeless Dragon, Li usually resides in the salty seas, but occasionally can be found in Asia's marshes.

If you want to gain the blessings of these dragons, burn incense and offer prayers to them. In many parts of China, special pagodas exist where people can go to solicit protection and good fortune from dragons.

DESCENDANTS OF DRAGONS

Gorgeous, wise, and powerful dragons sometimes mate with humans—and when they do, they produce extraordinary offspring who become great rulers. Many Asian emperors believed they descended from dragons. Even the famous Japanese Emperor Hirohito supposedly traced his lineage back to an ancient dragon king, though it would be hard to prove that claim using modern DNA testing.

Nuwa, the Chinese Snake Goddess

 nake deities and creation myths appear together in the legends of myriad cultures, including that of the Chinese. Legends credit the god Pan Gu with separating the heavens and the earth—but without the hard work of the Snake Goddess Nuwa none of it would have survived.

Often depicted as a half-human, half-snake—like the Hindu naginis—the beautiful goddess Nuwa plays a prominent role in mythology. She rescued China from total destruction when the spirit Gong Gong caused a mountain in the east to collapse. That continental sagging, by the way, shifted China's rivers so that ever after they've flowed eastward.

Chaos reigned when heaven's four pillars, which once supported the world, crumbled—until Nuwa stepped in to save the day. Using her feminine creative skills and ability to deal with whatever the universe threw at her, this ingenious goddess cut the legs off a huge tortoise and used them to prop up the four corners of the sky while she reinforced the structure with colored stones.

Once she'd stabilized the universe, Nuwa decided to marry—and she chose her brother Fuxi as her husband. Even in those long-ago times, the pair realized this incestuous match-up might be frowned upon. But the gods gave their okay and the couple became the parents of humankind. Nuwa commenced to populate the world she'd saved from ruin by first creating the animals and birds. Next she molded yellow clay into humanoid forms and people were born. After Nuwa had finished fashioning human beings, Fuxi stepped in and taught them to hunt, domesticate livestock, farm, read, and write.

A CHINESE CADUCEUS?

Chinese artwork often depicts the deities Nuwa and Fuxi as hybrid creatures with human torsos and serpentine lower bodies. As partners in the creation of the world, they frequently appear with their snaky tails entwined in a pattern reminiscent of the caduceus.

MIGRATING NAGAS AND NAGINIS

When Buddhism migrated to China, Tibet, Korea, Cambodia, and other parts of Asia, nagas and naginis did, too. India's Vedic tradition regards these human-snake hybrids as nature spirits and deities who bring good fortune as well as destruction to earthlings. In other countries, the nagas and naginis take on various qualities. The Cambodians believe they descended from these supernatural beings, born from the union of the naga king's daughter and the king of ancient Cambodia. A Tibetan legend says that long ago the land lay underwater and was ruled by the naga king. The naga, a disciple of the Buddha, dried up the land so a temple and monastery could be built there.

Pearl Diving "Mermaids"

or 1,500 years, Japanese women divers have plunged into the ocean's depths in search of shellfish, edible seaweed, and pearls. These amazing women reportedly dive down as far as 100 feet, traditionally wearing nothing but loincloths—no scuba gear—even in wintery water that's only 50°F. Nowadays, however, modern divers don facemasks and flippers, and in Korea they are permitted to wear wetsuits.

These aquatic athletes can hold their breath for more than three minutes and often continue to pursue their careers until they are sixty years old. Women, because their bodies contain more subcutaneous fat, can endure colder temperatures for longer periods than men can. Women can also dive deeper than men, without relying on air tanks.

It's possible that early sailors mistook these hardy and hardworking women for mermaids. In the mid-seventeenth century, a Dutch sailor whose ship wrecked in Korean waters spent nearly a year on the island of Cheju. There he had an opportunity to observe the topless female divers. When he returned home, he wrote a book about his experiences—including the Cheju "mermaids."

DRAGON WIVES

Interestingly, in Japan and China the word for mermaid means "dragon wife," signifying their awesome powers. Korea's divers are said to be more assertive than other women so the title is accurate.

"The girl cocked her head the other way.
I caught a glimpse of pink gills under her
chin. 'My sisters told me stories of humans.
They said they sometimes sing to them
to lure them underwater.' She grinned,
showing off her sharp needle-teeth.
'I've been practicing. Want to hear?'"

—Julie Kagawa, *The Iron King*

CHAPTER 10

Mermaids OF THE South Seas AND Australia

YOU'D EXPECT THE SOUTH SEAS from Hawaii to New Zealand to be swarming with mermaids—those lush, tropical islands, coral reefs, and sparkling blue waters seem like the perfect place for merfolk to frolic. Oddly, that's not the case. What we do find, though, are stories of water gods and goddesses—some with fish, snake, lizard, or crocodile appendages. These aquatic deities bear similarities to merfolk and water spirits in other parts of the world—they create and destroy life, they change themselves into people when they want to walk on land, and sometimes they marry human beings. As the South Sea islanders sailed from place to place, they took their legends with them. Over the centuries, their folktales have mixed, morphed, and emerged as delightfully diverse as the people who tell them.

Hawaii's Mo'o Goddesses

owerful Hawaiian water spirits known as the mo'o have a penchant for shapeshifting—from divine lizards to human women to goddesses. These magical females can assume whatever form they choose, from tiny geckos small enough to hold in the palm of your hand to giant lizard-ladies measuring thirty feet or more in length. Legends say the mo'o live in both fresh and saltwater—lakes and ponds, waterfalls and lagoons, as well as the ocean. Some sources link them with Chinese dragons or saltwater alligators.

Like mermaids, the mo'o can be dangerous—especially to men. Men simply can't resist the charms of these enchanting seductresses. But once the mo'o have won the affection of their human lovers, they drown the unsuspecting guys.

Many Hawaiians believe there's a little mo'o in every Hawaiian woman. Local lore tells us that human beings descended from these reptilian deities and sometimes important people transform into mo'o goddesses after death. That's what legend says happened to the sixteenth-century princess Kihawahine Mokuhinia Kalama'ula Kala'aiheana—when she died she became the mo'o goddess Kihawahine. So respected was Kihawahine that Hawaii's King Kamehameha I adopted her as his favorite goddess and allied himself with her descendants, knowing this would enhance his power and prestige.

Why are the mo'o so highly revered? Perhaps there's a connection between the mo'o—indeed, all snake deities—and the kundalini serpent of Hindu mystical tradition. Kundalini uses the coiled serpent to symbolize primal life energy and describes it as lying coiled at the base of the human spine. Without these spiritual serpents, we wouldn't be alive!

THE TIME DRAGON

In *Ho'opono: A Night Rainbow Book*, authors Pali Jae Lee and John K. Willis present an interesting way of seeing the mo'o as a "time dragon" that depicts a family's lineage. Using this method, the mo'o dragon becomes a genealogical symbol of past, present, and future generations. The bones, which form the mythical creature's structure, represent the ancestors. The head and eyes, which lead the dragon forward, signify future generations. Its front legs relate to the children, and the rest of its body represents the parents and grandparents. The tail, at the very back end of the dragon, symbolizes the distant past: "Aumakua," the family's spirit and divine source.

Siren Sightings

In 1838, thousands of people on the island of Maui reported seeing a lizard goddess named Moko-hinia at the funeral of a Hawaiian chief.

The Mo'o in the Wailuku River

eep in a cave at the bottom of Hawaii's beautiful Rainbow Falls lived the water spirit Hina, according to Hawaiian folklore. One day, a troublesome giant lizard deity called Mo'o Kuna conjured a ferocious storm that pushed a huge rock over the falls into Hawaii's longest river, the Wailuku. The boulder dammed the river, causing the water to rise to a dangerous level, threatening Hina's home.

Hina called to her son, Maui, for help, and he rushed to split the boulder. Then Maui chased after the malicious Mo'o Kuna in his canoe. He tried to spear the mo'o, but the crafty spirit hid in the river's waterholes and eluded him. So Maui petitioned the powerful fire goddess Pele to pour lava into the river. When the bubbling lava flowed into the river it made the water boil, which killed Mo'o Kuna. Victorious, Maui tossed the evil spirit's body over the falls.

It's said that Maui's canoe now rests in a lava channel in the Wailuku River—and if you look into the pool at the base of Rainbow Falls you can still see what remains of the mo'o. The Boiling Pots at the Wailuku River State Park represent the spot where the lava destroyed Mo'o Kuna—during storms the water in these holes looks as if it's actually boiling.

Zoologists doubt that huge physical lizards like Mo'o Kuna actually lived in Hawaii. However, visitors to Wailuku River State Park are warned "to be respectful of pools of water within the river—a favorite resting place of the mo'o."

A Legend of Mismatched Lovers

ina and Maui also turn up in the folklore of New Zealand, and according to one legend Hina was a beautiful young woman who lived on New Zealand's coast. One night she noticed a handsome man swimming in the ocean not far away and instantly fell in love with him. His name was Tuna, and the couple vowed to be together as husband and wife.

But Tuna had a secret side, and made his beloved promise never to search into his past or try to discover where he lived. In addition, she had to agree to only meet him at night.

After a while, the mystery and the limitations of the relationship frustrated and saddened Hina. Seeing Hina's unhappiness, the fisherman/divinity Maui approached her. Maui, being familiar with the sea, knew Tuna's true identity—he was a merman.

That night, Maui waited by the sea until Tuna emerged from the water to visit his wife. Tuna, sensing danger lurking nearby, told Hina he feared for his life. He asked her to promise that if he were to die, she would cut off his head and plant it in the ground. A tree would grow from it, he said, and the fruit of the tree would resemble his face and his matted hair.

As Tuna made his way back to the ocean, Maui leapt from his hiding place and killed the merman. Hina kept her promise and planted her husband's head, from which grew the majestic coconut palm tree. Each time she picked a coconut, she saw Tuna's head in her hands.

Variations on a Theme

 umerous stories of Hina, Tuna, and Maui exist in the folklore of Hawaii, Tahiti, and the many other islands in the South Seas. The people of the different islands give these legends their own, unique spin.

In some tales, Hina is considered a moon goddess and Tuna an eel-deity; in others Hina appears as a water goddess. In some versions, Maui buries the head of Tuna from which the coconut palm grew. Samoan legends speak of a girl-goddess named "Sina" and in their language "Tuna" means eel. One version of the folktale describes Tuna as her pet, rather than her husband. Others say Hina grew tired of Tuna and took Maui as her lover. In still other stories, Maui is Hina's son.

We find many Hinas in Hawaiian lore. Some describe her as a goddess, others as a woman. In some tales she lives in a cave behind a waterfall on the island of Maui, where she makes cloth from bark. A few of the Hina deities include:

- ≈ Hina lua lim kala, a beautiful mermaid who lives at the bottom of the ocean and heals with remedies gleaned from the sea.
- ≈ Hina 'opu hala ko'a, who presides over the coral reefs and spiny sea creatures.
- ≈ Hina puku i'a, the goddess of fishermen.

Maui also has many faces in old legends. Some stories describe him as a composite fisherman/divinity, whose mother threw him into the ocean at birth, leaving him to be raised by the sea itself. The various tales can get quite confusing—but no matter which version you hear, it's sure to be colorful and entertaining.

FIGHTING FISH

If you're a fish, humans are your enemy—they catch you and eat you, and they pollute your watery homes with their waste. A Maori legend tells of a great battle in which the creatures of the sea came on land and attacked human beings, led by the ocean god Tangaroa. The fish won the fight, and to reward them, Tangaroa allowed each of the sea creatures to choose a distinguishing feature. The swordfish opted for a sword, the octopus chose suctioned tentacles, and so on.

Mermaid Moana-Nui-Ka-Lehua

n Polynesian folklore, human beings and deities frequently intermingle. They also shapeshift at times— gods and goddesses take on human forms, and people change into divinities. Sometimes they even transform into trees and other life forms.

That's what happened to a mermaid/water goddess named Moana-Nui-Ka-Lehua, who lived in the ocean between the Hawaiian islands of K'aui and O'ahu. There she guarded the Ka'ie'ie Channel, with the aid of the two shark gods Kua and Kahole-a-Kane. Sometimes she appeared as a great fish, sometimes as a woman or a hybrid creature. Like many mermaids and water spirits, Moana-Nui-Ka-Lehua could whip up storms at sea in order to get what she wanted. One of her most famous incidents occurred when the volcano/fire goddess Pele fell in love with a mere mortal named Lohiau. Moana-Nui-Ka-Lehua brewed a tempest to prevent the couple from crossing the channel to marry.

But legend says the mermaid goddess met her match in the fisherman god Maui (who appears in the legends of many South Sea islanders). One day she discovered him fishing in her waters. To thwart him, she snagged his fishhook on a submerged rock.

Maui, a trickster figure in mythology, wasn't about to be undone so easily. He pursued the mermaid until he captured her. Then he brought her ashore, where she died. However, Maui showed respect for his antagonist—he laid her body to rest on a shrine. Moana-Nui-Ka-Lehua's spirit transformed into an ohi'a lehua, one of Hawaii's most common trees.

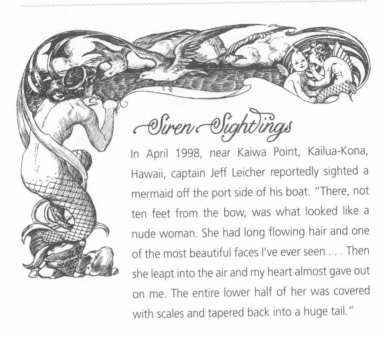

Siren Sightings

In April 1998, near Kaiwa Point, Kailua-Kona, Hawaii, captain Jeff Leicher reportedly sighted a mermaid off the port side of his boat. "There, not ten feet from the bow, was what looked like a nude woman. She had long flowing hair and one of the most beautiful faces I've ever seen . . . Then she leapt into the air and my heart almost gave out on me. The entire lower half of her was covered with scales and tapered back into a huge tail."

Tangaroa, the Sea-God

 ong ago, says Polynesian mythology, the Earth was an arid mass, devoid of water. That's because the creator earth-goddess Papatuanuku (Papa) held all the water inside her body. But in time, she could no longer contain it all—her body burst and the oceans of the world spilled out.

She granted her son Tangaroa dominion over the newly formed seas and all the creatures in them—including mermaids and mermen. According to legend, Tangaroa is so enormous that he only breathes once per day—and his inhalation and exhalation cause the tides to rise and fall. Tangaroa has a brother named Rongo, who some stories say is the equivalent of the fisherman/god Maui, and his grandchildren are the ancestors of the reptiles and the fish. When the weather is pleasant, it's said that Tangaroa turns into a big, green lizard.

Although renowned throughout the South Seas as a powerful creator spirit, fertility deity, and ocean god, Tangaroa plays many roles and assumes many guises, as often happens in island myths.

- ≈ The Samoans and Tongalese know him as the principal creator deity, who ruled over the ocean. He tossed rocks into the sea to form Samoa and Tonga.
- ≈ The Tahitians call him Ta'aroa and consider him the main creator god. Supposedly he emerged from a cosmic egg and from the broken shell he formed the Earth and the sky.
- ≈ The Hawaiians named him Kanaloa, and associate him with squid and octopi.
- ≈ The Maori say Tangaroa formed human beings from maggots.

The relationships between these water deities and merfolk is as complex and mysterious as the ocean itself. Perhaps that's why we find them so fascinating.

ANCESTRAL MERMAIDS

Polynesian mythology says human beings evolved from the merfolk. According to local legend, people gradually lost their fishy qualities over time and adapted to living on land.

Sirenas

n the waters around the Philippine Islands, fishermen and sailors claim to have seen mermaids, as many people who live and work on the oceans do. Legends say Philippine mermaids, known as sirenas, look pretty much like the beautiful half-human, half-fish creatures we're familiar with.

But the males of the species don't necessarily mirror the comely qualities of their female counterparts. Some mermen, called siyokoy, do sport human torsos and the usual fishtails below the abdomen. Their brown or gray skin resembles that of fish and they have gills through which they breathe—some of them even have tentacles, like squid. Others, though, look pretty much like men but with scaly legs and webbed feet.

At the top of the Philippine's merfolk hierarchy come the kataw, who lack the typical merman's fishtail. These sea-guys can pass for humans—and often do. If you look closely, though, you'll notice their gills and the finny forms attached to their arms. The kataws control the waters around the islands—the tides, currents, and the movements of the aquatic creatures.

Fishermen fear the kataw—unlike the more benevolent Sirena, who serves as goddess of the fish. Legend says the kataw pretends to be an ordinary fisherman and when he comes upon a human he feigns being in need of assistance. When the real fisherman goes to his aid, the kataw either drowns him and/or eats the unsuspecting Good Samaritan.

Australia's Yawkyawk

"Some features of a respective country are equated with body parts of Yawkyawk. For example a bend in a river or creek may be said to be the tail of the Yawkyawk, a billabong may be the head of the Yawkyawk, and so on. Thus different groups can be linked together by means of a shared mythology featured in the landscape, which crosscuts clan and language group boundaries."

—Felicity Green (ed.), *Togart Contemporary Art Award (NT) 2007*, exhibition catalogue

n Australia's streams and ponds live the spirits of young girls, say the Kuninjku people. At night, you can sometimes see their shadowy forms scurrying across the landscape, for these water spirits—known as yawkyawk—usually steer clear of human beings. If you catch more than a glimpse of one, you'll notice her upper body looks human enough, but below the waist she's a fish.

The yawkyawk, sometimes referred to as *ngalberddjenj*, which means "the young woman who has a tail like a fish," are said to have long green hair that resembles seaweed. But when they want to come on land (usually at night) they sprout legs and seem to be wholly human. Some legends insist yawkyawk can even transform themselves into dragonflies. Others describe them with the appendages of snakes or crocodiles.

As water spirits, the yawkyawk control the rains, and everything depends on them bringing life-giving water. Most of the time, these beautiful creatures exhibit temperate dispositions—but when they get angry, they can conjure up storms just like other mermaids. Like most water deities, yawkyawk are linked with fertility and creation—they're so powerful, it's said, that women need only go near the streams and pools where the spirits live to become pregnant.

Occasionally, a yawkyawk marries a human being (who may or may not realize what she really is). But after a time, she grows tired of the world of people and returns to her watery abode.

JOURNEY OF THE YAWKYAWK

Australia's Aborigines believe animals started out as human beings—not the other way around, as Darwin's theory suggests. Over time, they evolved into the myriad animals we know today. But not all of them made the transition completely. Among those that remain in between are the hybrid yawkyawk.

The Australian Rainbow Serpent

he indigenous people of Australia speak of deities known as Rainbow Serpents. The female, Yingarna, is the original creator deity; the male, Ngalyod, transformed the land from a flat plain to a continent with hills and rivers. Some folktales describe them as the parents of the yawkyawk; others claim the spirits are the same, they just appear in different forms—as shapeshifting divinities are known to do. Legend says the serpents usually live in Australia's water holes beneath waterfalls, but can be found in other bodies of water as well.

To the Aborigines, the Rainbow Serpents represent fertility and abundance because of their ability to bring rain. But when the serpents become angry, they punish human beings with storms and floods—typical of water deities' dual powers of creation and destruction. To be on the safe side, the Aborigines hold ritual celebrations to honor and appease the serpent, using quartz crystals to fragment the sun's light into the colors of the rainbow.

Like other creator-destroyer spirits, the Rainbow Serpent can heal or wreak havoc for humans. Shamans (medicine men) are believed to receive their magical powers from the Rainbow Serpent. One legend says that the snake can enter a person's body, where it leaves "little rainbows" that can cause illness and death. But if, after several days of sickness, a healer removes the offending spirits from the patient, the person will recover and become a healer himself.

 WEIRD AND WILD

Archaeologists have found rock paintings of the Rainbow Serpent in the Arnhem Land of Australia dating back 6,000 years. A strange and colorful composite of creatures, the Rainbow Serpent is sometimes depicted as a snake with pieces of kangaroos, foxes, crocodiles, or other animals mixed in. From its head stream long locks of human hair.

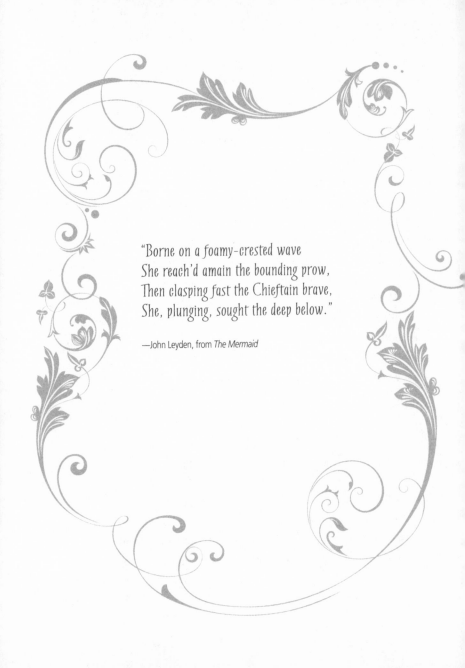

"Borne on a foamy-crested wave
She reach'd amain the bounding prow,
Then clasping fast the Chieftain brave,
She, plunging, sought the deep below."

—John Leyden, from *The Mermaid*

CHAPTER 11

Mermaids of North and South America

LONG BEFORE EUROPEAN SAILORS came to the New World, bringing fantastic tales of mermaids with them, the indigenous peoples of the Americas already told stories of fish-women who lived in the oceans, rivers, and lakes. Other legends, including those of the Haitians' Lasirèn (whose name means mermaid in French), migrated to their present locales when African slaves were brought to the Caribbean and North America.

Modern-day mermaids in the United States are more playful than powerful. In cartoons and children's books, at carnivals and celebrations such as New York's bawdy Coney Island Mermaid Parade and the kitschy Las Vegas Mermaid Convention, mermaids entertain us rather than govern our lives. Merchandisers have denatured the fearsome and formidable sirens of old and repackaged them as frivolous toys—still stunningly beautiful, but harmless. Yet the mermaid mystique remains in the human psyche and despite contemporary attempts to tame the wild sea goddess, in the end we know she's more than just a pretty face—and that keeps us in her thrall.

Passamaquoddy Mermaids

 any years ago, a Passamaquoddy man and woman lived by the sea in what is now New Brunswick. They had two daughters who loved to swim, but the mother, knowing the perils of the ocean, feared something dreadful might happen to them and forbade the girls to go in the water. As teenagers are inclined to do, the girls disobeyed their mother and swam in secret, stripping off their clothes to enjoy the sensual feel of the water on their bare skin.

One day the girls didn't come home. Their parents went searching for them and found their discarded clothing on the beach. Gazing out to sea, they spotted their daughters floating on the waves and called to them. The girls swam toward shore, but when they drew near they realized they couldn't climb out of the water—their bodies had grown too heavy for them to walk.

When they looked down into the water, the sisters saw that their lower bodies had changed into slimy fishtails—they'd spent so much time in the water that they'd transformed into mermaids. The man and woman tried to gather up their daughters' clothing, but the girls sang out in melodious voices, telling their parents not to bother—they weren't coming back to live on land again. The mother started crying, but her daughters comforted her, insisting they were content.

From then on, whenever the man and woman went out in their canoe, their mermaid daughters pushed it along, enabling the parents to go anyplace they liked, effortlessly and safely.

Squant, the Sea-Woman

"When the tide came in again, she drifted along with it, and this time she smiled. The storm went away; the wind blew from the south; the sun came out; and Maushop saw that her hair was green, glistening, her body wide and flat like a ribbon of kelp. He knew then, that she was Squant, the sea-giantess."

 —E. Reynard, *The Narrow Land*

n the days when giants lived among us, one named Maushop resided by the ocean at Popponesset, on what is now Cape Cod, Massachusetts. Among Indians, Maushop was revered for killing a bird-monster who devoured children. After he destroyed the demon, a terrible storm arose and huge waves broke on the shore—bringing with them a sea-woman. Her long, green hair resembled tangled seaweed and her fingers and toes were webbed. Over the roar of the waves, Maushop could hear her singing and he recognized her as Squant, the Sea Goddess.

Each day after that, Squant visited Maushop on the incoming tide. Sometimes he swam in the sea with her, but no matter how she tempted him with her captivating smile and her enchanting songs, he knew better than to go with her to her underwater cave. And though he desired her, he would not forsake his wife and children. When Maushop refused to follow the sea-woman, the furious Squant made the seas churn with thundering waves and filled the air with icy winds.

Then one day Maushop caught his wife with another man and, in his anger, threw her and his children into the ocean. The children changed into fish and swam away.

The giant returned to the spot where Squant had visited him and sat gazing out at the ocean. Soon, the sea-woman rose on the waves, blowing bubbles and singing. She shook her green hair and again invited him to join her in her cave beneath the sea. This time, when the tide ebbed, he followed her—never to return.

Salmon Boy

 or the Haida Indians, who live in British Columbia, salmon is a major source of food—so it makes sense that among their legends we'd find a story of salmon-human merfolk. In one folktale, a young Haida boy went swimming in a river with his friends—but the current swept him underwater and he drowned before his companions could save him. As his body sunk, the salmon captured his soul and took it to their underwater home.

Shapeshifting is a popular theme in Native American legends—and among merfolk generally—and once the salmon reached their home at the bottom of the river, they changed into people. The boy magically came back to life. The salmon-people, he learned, ate human children who swam in the river—just as human beings caught and ate salmon from the river.

One day while fishing, the boy's mother snagged her salmon-son on her hook and recognized him by his necklace. She laid the fish on the ground and soon the boy's head poked out of the salmon's mouth. Before long, the boy himself emerged from the fish, leaving its scaly skin behind. The boy then assumed the role of medicine man or shaman to his tribe and taught them the "way of the salmon."

Late in life, the salmon-shaman caught a fish—but not just any fish, it was his own soul. When he killed the fish, he died as well. His tribesmen returned the old shaman's body to the river, which symbolized the cycle of death and rebirth.

A Tale of a Twin-Tailed Merman

egends often arise from real-life events, handed down through oral tradition from generation to generation. This colorful story tells of the Shawnee's migration from Pennsylvania, Ohio, and Indiana to the Midwest—guided by a merman.

According to folklore, a strange and captivating creature appeared to the Eastern Shawnee, the likes of which they'd never seen before. The creature resembled a man, but with green hair and a slimy beard, and he sailed across the surface of a great lake astride the back of a huge fish. The man wore seashells around his neck. When the fish leapt from the water, the people could see the peculiar man's lower body—where his legs should have been they saw two fish-like appendages instead!

In a tantalizing voice, the merman sang of a lush and lovely land beyond the sea, tempting the Shawnee with promises of a better life. So mesmerized were the people that they ceased their usual activities and sat on the shore, listening to the merman. At first they hesitated to follow him, but the charming creature reminded them of the harsh winters and dangers they faced in their present home. He sang sweetly of a warmer land where deer and buffalo proliferated, and eventually convinced them.

The Shawnee climbed into their boats and paddled for two moons, guided by the merman. Finally they reached their new home, a beautiful place with fertile earth and abundant game. The merman bid them farewell, and the people thrived—just as the strange man-fish guide had promised.

Sedna, the Sea Goddess

 o the Inuit, Sedna is the most powerful of deities, the sea goddess whose sacrifice brought abundant food to her people. But before Sedna became a goddess she was a beautiful young Inuit woman whom many men fancied. She refused them all and instead married a trickster seabird who promised her a wonderful life on an island. Soon, Sedna discovered that life on the island was nothing like her husband had described—in fact, it was dreadful.

So Sedna's father rowed his boat to the island, where he killed her lying bird-husband and rescued Sedna. On the way back, however, the bird's friends summoned a great storm that threatened to drown father and daughter. Terrified, Sedna's father threw his daughter overboard. When she tried to hold onto the side of the boat, he chopped off her fingers. Sedna sank beneath the water, where she metamorphosed into a sea goddess with the upper body and head of a woman and the tail or a whale or fish. Her fingers became the fish, seals, and whales that make up the Inuit's diet.

It's said that so long as the Inuit people pay respect to Sedna and honor her with festivals and offerings, she will continue to provide for them. If they disobey or neglect her, however, she'll show her anger by causing terrible storms that make fishing impossible, depriving the people of food.

UPDATING SEDNA'S IMAGE

Sedna usually appears as a typical mermaid today. But it's possible that whalers brought that image with them, carved as figureheads on their ships when they came to the Arctic regions. Earlier Inuit folktales described Sedna as a human woman, rather than a hybrid being.

HOW TO WIN SEDNA'S FAVOR

Legend says that an Inuit shaman who wants Sedna to bless his people can play the role of divine beautician to the sea goddess. He must swim to the bottom of the ocean with a comb in hand. Once there, his job is to comb her long hair and braid it. It seems that Sedna, like most mermaids, enjoys being pampered.

The Mermaid of Gocta Cataracts

eru's Gocta Cataracts, one of the world's tallest waterfalls, drops 2,531 feet into a beautiful dark pool where local legend says a wish-granting mermaid lives. Until recently, few outsiders even knew this majestic falls existed, but according to local legend, a poor fisherman named Gregorio who once lived near the remote waterfall befriended the mermaid there and often spoke with her.

One day the mermaid offered to grant a wish for Gregorio—he could have anything he wanted. The modest fisherman asked only for a good day of fishing. The lovely mermaid fulfilled her promise and gave him a huge bag of fish to take home. That night his wife began cleaning the fish—and discovered a gold ring among them. Quickly she pocketed the ring, without mentioning it to Gregorio.

When Gregorio visited the mermaid again, the same thing happened. Once more, the fisherman wished only for a good catch and the mermaid granted his wish. This time, Gregorio's wife found a gold bracelet in the bag with the fish, and hid it from her husband.

Afraid that Gregorio had stolen the jewelry, his wife followed him to Gocta Cataracts the next day. There, at the bottom of the falls, she saw her husband talking with a most unusual woman. Her upper body was silver and below the waist she wore a fishtail of glimmering gold. When the mermaid spotted Gregorio's wife, she grabbed the fisherman and dove into the pool, taking him with her. The wife ran to the water's edge, but Gregorio had disappeared entirely, never to return.

Lasirèn, the Vodou Mermaid

"The mermaid, the whale,
My hat falls into the sea.
I caress the mermaid,
My hat falls into the sea.
I lie down with the mermaid,
My hat falls into the sea."

 —Haitian Vodou chant

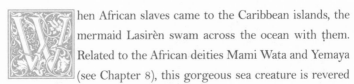 hen African slaves came to the Caribbean islands, the mermaid Lasirèn swam across the ocean with them. Related to the African deities Mami Wata and Yemaya (see Chapter 8), this gorgeous sea creature is revered in the Vodou tradition of Haiti and New Orleans. Magical and mysterious, she's a composite of dark and light, a symbol of the union of opposites—as such, she may appear either with light or dark skin,

fair or black hair. Sometimes artists depict her as a beautiful mulatto woman with green eyes and straight black hair—an enchanting blend of the black and white races.

Legend says that if you see Lasirèn, you're about to receive a profound and sudden insight, one that might even change your life. That's the meaning of the line "My hat falls into the sea" in the chant above, for the sea represents intuition and the unconscious. Like mermaids everywhere, Lasirèn carries a mirror and comb, but her mirror is more than an object of vanity. Symbolically, it represents a portal between the conscious and unconscious worlds, urging us to look within as well as without in order to "see" ourselves more clearly.

Like other mermaids, Lasirèn likes to grab humans and take them to her underwater home—a luxurious palace decked out with treasure from sunken ships. But unlike most mermaids, she prefers to capture women. Some drown, but those who return have learned from Lasirèn how to heal and see into the future.

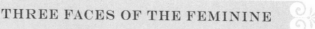

THREE FACES OF THE FEMININE

In Haitian mythology, Lasirèn had two sisters, Danto and Freda. Together the three represent three faces of the feminine: mother, lover, and goddess. Lasirèn's sister Danto symbolized the mother, the cool, calm female who's responsible and in control. Sister Freda signifies the lover—sexy, passionate, and temperamental. Lasirèn depicts the goddess, the mystical, spiritual aspect of a woman.

Celebrating Lasirèn

f you're looking for prosperity, love, health, or good luck, you may want to petition the lovely Lasirèn, the mermaid-goddess of the Haitian people. To gain her favor, Vodou's followers fill small boats with offerings to Lasirèn and set them afloat—she especially likes jewelry, flowers, wine, doves, perfume, combs, and mirrors. Some say Lasirèn's spirit enters the bodies of women and brings them good fortune in all areas of life, especially in love.

The Haitians also hold elaborate processions in Lasirèn's honor. Male celebrants carry a seductive woman, who represents the mermaid, through the streets—for of course, she can't walk with that glistening green tail instead of legs—while the adoring crowds sing, chant, and cheer to her. In addition to her mermaid garb, the lady wears sparkling baubles and beads to symbolize the riches she can bestow on those who believe in her. Naturally, she combs her luxurious long hair while gazing into her mirror. Sometimes she blows a trumpet—another of Lasirèn's symbols—or a conch shell, like the Greek merman Triton. To keep this sea-goddess comfortable while she's on land, her followers bathe her with water along the route.

Exquisite banners, tapestries, and flags are a colorful part of Lasirèn ceremonies. Each handmade satin banner features the image of a saint or *iwa*, created from sequins and sparkling beads—as many as 10,000 on a single banner. Vodou's followers carry the banners at the head of processions and hang the sacred flags from churches where the deities will be sure to see them.

Summer Spectacle

 estive, funky, and lots of fun, the Mermaid Parade on Coney Island is New York's answer to Mardi Gras and Carnival. Begun in 1983 to "pay homage to Coney Island's forgotten Mardi Gras," the parade's founders say it "celebrates the sand, the sea, the salt air and the beginning of summer, as well as the history and mythology of Coney Island." It's also the perfect opportunity to play mermaid for a day—or to ogle the throngs of scantily clad females decked out in shells, sequins, fishtails, and body paint.

The wonderfully whacky celebration, billed by Coney Island as "the nation's largest art parade and one of New York City's greatest events," welcomes in summer on the Saturday closest to the summer solstice. Marching bands, crazy floats, hot air balloons, and mermaids of every imaginable type parade down Surf Avenue in a vibrant display of creative self-expression. Each year two celebrities preside over the spectacle as Queen Mermaid and King Neptune. In the past, Queen Latifah, Lou Reed, David Byrne, Laurie Anderson, and Harvey Keitel have filled the fishtails of the royal couple. The nonprofit event draws thousands of participants who vie for prizes and hundreds of thousands of onlookers each year.

A zany ball follows the parade, where mermaids, mermen, and sea creatures mingle with mere mortals to eat, drink, and make merry. The party includes burlesque and circus acts featuring live "mermaids" cavorting with aquatic animals, along with music, dancing, and revelry to rival San Francisco's Castro Street Fair. For photos and information visit *www.coneyisland.com*.

Siren Sightings

Oregon writer D. J. Conway is certain she saw a real mermaid. In *Magickal Mermaids and Water Creatures* she writes, "I have seen only one mermaid personally, and because I had binoculars there was no doubt what the being was. Clearly I saw the long pale flash of arms and head as the mermaid leaped and played in the waves. Each time she went beneath the water, her iridescent fish tail was very visible. In her last dive, she smacked the ocean with her tail as if laughing at my astonishment."

Making a Splash

as Vegas may seem like an odd place to find mermaids, considering the glitzy gambling capital is a long way from the ocean. But on the weekend of August 12–13, 2011, hundreds of mermaids and mermen showed up for the first Mermaid Convention and World Mermaid Awards or "MerCon" at the city's Silverton Hotel and Casino. Glamorous mermaids of all ages from around the globe competed in a variety of categories, dressed in shell-bras and slinky, sparkly tails. Obviously mermaids can't walk, so each contestant was carried onto the stage. Mermen and even merchildren participated for awards. Juliana Tucker, who performs at Walt Disney World in Orlando, Florida, won the coveted title of Miss International Mermaid.

A huge pool party followed, at which famous professional mermaid Hannah, a.k.a. "Hannah Mermaid" (who makes a living swimming with sharks and whales) performed her underwater acrobatics—diving, twirling, and doing all sorts of graceful mermaid moves. Sita Lange of the Maui Mermaids organized the wild and whacky charitable event to raise money for Purity of Water, a nonprofit organization dedicated to cleaning up and protecting the waters of the world.

Guest judge Carolyn Turgeon, author of the novel *Mermaid*, deemed the weekend-long affair—complete with fire-spinning mermaids, hula girls, and belly dancers—"beautiful and ridiculous, which all the best things are, especially when you're in Las Vegas." To see footage of the event, visit the *Las Vegas Review-Journal*'s website at *www.lvrj.com*.

"[H]e would come up with mermaid scales still sticking to him, and yet not be able to say for certain what had been happening. It was really rather irritating to children who had never seen a mermaid."

—J. M. Barrie, *Peter Pan*

A SHAWL FOR COLD MERMAIDS

Do mermaids, nude to the waist and exposed to the elements, ever get chilly? If so, artist/author Kathleen Valentine has designed the perfect cover-up for these half-naked ladies: the "mermaid shawl." A gorgeous, lacy wrap with a shell-like motif knitted in the soft hues of the sea, it wraps mermaids or human females in luxury, from their graceful shoulders down to their pretty round bottoms. Valentine's popular book, *The Mermaid Shawl & Other Beauties*, provides patterns and instructions to help knitters create their own works of art.

Under the Sea

isney had a thing for mermaids long before the hit animated film *The Little Mermaid* captured the hearts of moviegoers. In the summer of 1959, Disneyland introduced an attraction called Submarine Voyage, which featured eight live mermaids doing a water ballet in the park's lagoon. Visitors climbed into mini-submarines, designed to resemble World War II nuclear subs that held thirty-two people, and slowly navigated the lagoon. Through the submarines' porthole windows they could watch the lovely waving mermaids swim past, accompanied by colorful fish.

In 1965, the mermaids returned to celebrate Disneyland's tenth anniversary. The aquatic beauties were such a hit with visitors that Submarine Voyage decided to invite them back the following summer. But in 1998, the ride made its last voyage and closed down.

Now, mermaid fans can again visit a magical underwater kingdom and cavort with sea creatures at Disneyland's new Little Mermaid ride, which opened in June 2011. The old submarines have been replaced with clamshell-shaped boats that take visitors to mermaid Ariel's colorful grotto. Spectacular special effects, music, and familiar characters from the movie greet guests and tell Ariel's story. When the teenage mermaid leaves her home at the bottom of the sea to begin her adventure on land, human visitors "ascend" with her—back to the real world. Finny fun for mermaids of all ages.

QUALIFICATIONS FOR A MERMAID

Aspiring mermaids for the original Disneyland Submarine Voyage had to stand between 5 feet 4 inches and 5 feet 7 inches tall, have long hair, and be able to swim well. It goes without saying that they had to be pretty, too. The mermaids swam, sunbathed, and waved to visitors for four hours a day. Except for the problem of getting green hair from the lagoon's water, ex-mermaid Shannon Baughmann called it a fin-tastic "dream job."

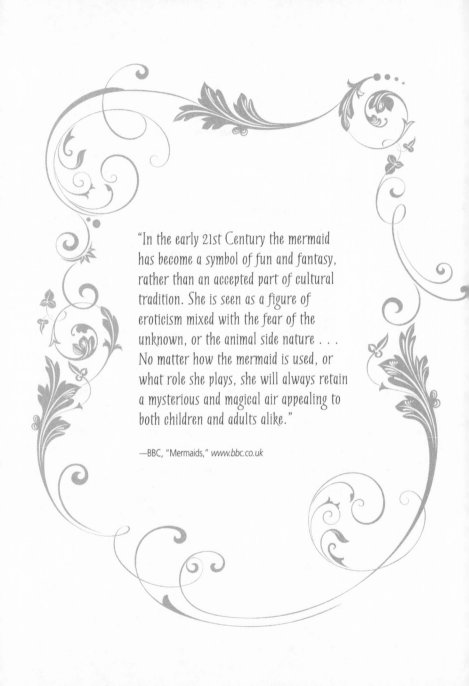

"In the early 21st Century the mermaid has become a symbol of fun and fantasy, rather than an accepted part of cultural tradition. She is seen as a figure of eroticism mixed with the fear of the unknown, or the animal side nature . . . No matter how the mermaid is used, or what role she plays, she will always retain a mysterious and magical air appealing to both children and adults alike."

—BBC, "Mermaids," *www.bbc.co.uk*

The *Hidden Meanings* of *Mermaids*

MERMAIDS HAVE FASCINATED and mystified us for millennia—so there must be something more to them than their pretty faces and figures. Symbols only endure if they touch upon a truth that resonates deep within us, a truth that is both personal and universal. Mythology and art frequently use symbols to convey meanings—especially in earlier times when most people couldn't read or write—and the mermaid is a provocative symbol, today as well as in the past.

What do mermaids have to say to us? You've learned a lot throughout this book, but let's take a second look at some of the symbolism attached to mermaids and the hidden messages these lovely ladies are trying to send us. As we do, let's also reflect back on the significance of mermaids through the ages and what we can learn from them today.

A Return to the Sea

"[Water] has always been a feminine symbol—it is natural that the water spirits should most often be symbolized as female."

—Manly P. Hall, *The Secret Teachings of All Ages*

cience tells us that all life on Earth evolved from the ocean, the "womb of the world." Not only is the sea home to the mermaid, it is our primordial home as well. When we see a mermaid riding happily on the waves, we're reminded of our origins. When she beckons us to follow her into her underwater realm, we feel, perhaps, a twinge of longing to return to the soothing, weightlessness of the womb where we once floated comfortably in a salty sea of amniotic fluid.

Our bodies—and especially our brains—contain a high percentage of water. So even though we can't breathe underwater, like mermaids do, we sense an affinity with water—it's as if we haven't entirely left our past behind. As a hybrid being, the mermaid symbolizes our transformation from fish to Homo sapiens. We identify with her because, like the mermaid, we're still partly creatures of the sea.

Early people linked not only mermaids but also goddesses with the waters of the world. The oceans, rivers, and lakes provided nourishment—without them, human beings couldn't survive. These potent goddesses held the power of life and death in their hands. Our ancestors honored the water deities, seeking to win their favor and their life-giving blessings. Over time, their majesty was transferred to mermaids. Like the sea itself, mermaids could bring good fortune or devastation. That mysterious power still entices us today.

Sensual Sirens

o one can deny the sexual allure of the mermaid. Even Disney's cute cartoon character Ariel retains a not-so-subtle symbol of passion—her fiery red hair. Historically, hair has been associated with power, and a woman's hair represented sexual power specifically. Supposedly, men found women's hair so deliciously distracting that for centuries religions forbade females to display their tempting tresses publicly—and certainly not in church! In the prim and proper Victorian era, women bound up their hair, symbolically reining in their power and taming it, lest they drive men wild.

Beautiful, bare-breasted mermaids have tempted seamen for centuries. Virtually all legends describe mermaids as exquisitely good-looking, with perfectly shaped full breasts, silky-smooth skin, and the slim torsos of lovely young women. Their unabashed willingness to display their luscious bodies added to their appeal—especially when human females were extolled to keep theirs covered up. During the days when sailing ships still navigated the seas, painters weren't allowed to portray real women in the nude—but goddesses and mermaids could flaunt their naked glory with abandon.

If mermaids evolved from the early fertility goddesses, as many researchers believe, it's only natural for them to continue on as sex symbols. The Assyrian goddess Atargartis, who became our first mermaid, was an important fertility deity. So were the African goddesses Yemaja and Oshun, the Greeks' Aphrodite, and the Romans' Venus. To our ancestors, the female's ability to bring forth life gave her a magical power that made her absolutely awesome.

The Mermaid's Tail

hat's sexy about a fishtail? In *The Republic of Love*, Carol Shields describes it as "a sealed vessel enclosing either sexual temptation or sexual virtue, or some paradoxical and potent mixture of the two." In fact, part of the mermaid's appeal may be her sexual unattainability—we always want what we can't have. She's the ultimate tease. Here's this gorgeous babe with the breasts of a Playboy bunny, the face of an angel, and the long, flowing hair of a supermodel—but a man can never consummate a relationship with her because her tail prevents access to her "lady parts."

The mermaid's tail is one of her most obvious and intriguing symbols. But her tail didn't always look the way it does now. She wasn't always so restrained. As we discussed in Chapter 2, early depictions of mermaids often showed them with two tails or a tail split down the middle, suggesting that they could take on human lovers after all. Remember the first mermaid Starbucks used for its logo? That half-naked beauty was of the two-tailed variety and she provocatively parted her tails,

holding them up on either side of her bare torso, enticing customers with her charms.

The twin-tailed mermaid reminds us of the ancient Sheila-na-gig fertility goddesses of the pre-Christian Celts. This brazen and bawdy baubo deity squats to reveal her genitals as a symbol of feminine power. So it would seem that the early mermaid retained a close connection with the old fertility goddesses—and the creative power they possessed—which later versions attempted to diminish by cocooning her lower body in a single tail.

Beauty and Vanity

"Her mirror, later a symbol of her vanity, originally represented the planet Venus in astrological tradition. Her abundant, flowing hair, symbolizing an abundant love potential, was also an attribute of Venus in her role as fertility goddess."

—Scarlett deMason, "Shadows of the Goddess—The Mermaid"

lways looking in the mirror and combing her hair, the mermaid certainly strikes us as one vain female. Then there's her penchant for decking herself out in jewels—which some legends say she scavenged from the treasure chests of sunken ships. Of course, she's drop-dead gorgeous to begin with, as many a sailor will attest. But if her looks alone aren't enough to garner attention from passing seafarers, the mermaid sings out in the most enchanting voice until no man can resist her.

Vanity, as you recall, is one of the seven deadly sins, and early churches used the symbolism of the mermaid to remind the faithful of this fact. Comb-and-mirror-toting mermaids adorned many a sanctuary wall in medieval churches—frequently swimming among schools of fish, which symbolized Christianity. In a sixteenth-century Cornish church, a wooden pew features a carving of a mermaid holding her mirror and comb—a warning, perhaps, for legends say mermaids dragged many Cornwall men down to their deaths in the sea.

But you can't really blame mermaids for being such narcissists. Mythology says these fascinating females descended from the ancient goddesses of love and beauty: Aphrodite and Venus. These delectable deities governed art, music, poetry, love, and the finer things in life. It was their job not only to look good, but to enrich the world with beauty in all its many forms. And as we know too well, there's enough ugliness in the world—maybe we need mermaids to add a touch of glamour and grace.

THE MERMAID'S MAGIC MIRROR

Often considered a sign of vanity, the mermaid's mirror is a symbol of something else as well. Like magic mirrors everywhere, it gives her clairvoyant skills and lets her view the future. Thus, her mirror represents the ability to see through the "veil" that mystics say separates the visible and spirit worlds.

Creators and Destroyers

 istorically, mermaids represented danger. It wasn't until the Victorian era that they started appearing as fantasy friends in children's books and as nubile Lolitas on the walls of gentlemen's chambers.

Most legends and folklore portray mermaids as temptresses who lure human beings—mostly men—into the water and drown them. Other tales warn seafarers of the mermaid's capricious nature—she simply can't be trusted. She might protect sailors on their ocean voyages or brew up ferocious storms to sink their ships. You just never know.

The mermaid's song, mythology tells us, is one of her most seductive and deadly attributes. Ever since the Greek Sirens tormented Odysseus, mermaids have been singing men to sleep—permanently. Mermaids' enchanting voices mess with seamen's minds so intensely that they run their ships aground or jump, delirious, into the sea and perish.

But mermaids aren't all bad. Many of them, such as Japan's Benton, bring good luck and happiness to people. The Africans' Mami Wata provides food, shelter, and prosperity to human beings. Other mermaids, such as Oshun, heal the sick. The Warsaw mermaid serves as the city's protectress and benefactor. Folklore says that mermaids can grant wishes, too.

Mermaids follow in the footsteps of the ancient goddesses, who provided water for crops and food for people. But they also caused devastating storms and floods. The goddesses gave and the goddesses took away. The mermaid's dual nature actually adds to her allure. The combination of desirability and danger makes her infinitely intriguing—and for men who enjoy a challenge, she's irresistible.

Wise Women

 oday's mermaids may epitomize the "dumb blonde" image or appear as cute, cuddly playmates. But myths and folklore often present them as wise women with the power to heal, teach, and guide human beings. Ancient Sumerian myths say mermaids educated people and taught them science and the arts. The Babylonian merman Ea shared his knowledge of agriculture and architecture with humans. The Caribbean mermaid Lasirèn takes people underwater and gives them special powers, including psychic ability.

In myth and psychology, water symbolizes the emotions, intuition, and the unconscious. Because the mermaid lives in the water, she has access to these areas, whereas humans often ignore them.

The mermaid plumbs the ocean's depths—and the unconscious—bringing up treasure she finds at the bottom. Spiritual teachers and therapists advise that in order to be happy, healthy, and wise, we must get in touch with our emotions and our inner selves. The mermaid's ability to breathe underwater and to gracefully ride the ocean's waves indicates that she understands this very well.

Some legends describe mermaids with snaky appendages rather than fishtails. In mythology, snakes represent wisdom, transformation, and regeneration. To Hindus, serpents symbolize the life force. Folklore tells us that mermaids can shapeshift, too, changing themselves into fish, seals, snakes, birds, or humans—they're not limited to a single lifestyle or worldview. But no matter what form her lower body takes, the mermaid epitomizes the power to move between the worlds and to show us how to do it.

Changing the Mermaid's Image

 othing stays the same forever, and that goes for mermaids as well. Early mermaids evolved from the great water goddesses of the world—mighty feminine forces who governed the rise and fall of the tides, the flooding of the rivers, and the aquatic life that provided food for humankind. Like those goddesses, mermaids were viewed as dynamic and powerful creatures with tempestuous natures.

In the Middle Ages, the mermaid showed her bawdy side by separating her single tail into two parts, shamelessly revealing her female secrets. Despite their blatant sexuality, these split-tailed seductresses appear as decorations on medieval churches and cathedrals

LORD FREDERIC LEIGHTON, *THE FISHERMAN AND THE SIREN*

throughout Europe, the British Isles, and Ireland. They even adorn Bologna's fourteenth-century Fontana di Nettuno, which commemorated a pope's appointment.

During the Romantic and Victorian periods, in the latter part of the nineteenth century, mermaids mellowed into sensual sweeties reminiscent of the ancient Greek nymphs. Rather than terrifying men, these lovely lasses gazed demurely from the paintings of John William Waterhouse, Frederic Leighton, and others, promising pleasure without pain.

Today's mermaids are fun-loving and friendly. The frightening, destroyer sirens of the past have been ousted in favor of pleasure-seeking playmates. Their youthful abandon, grace, and sense of freedom invite us to lighten up. They remind us to enjoy life and glide through the waters of life, rather than struggling. Perhaps these bathing beauties are just what we need now to help us escape from the stress of the modern world and our anxiety about the future.

Bibliography

Andersen, Hans Christian. *The Little Mermaid*, 1836. (*http://hca.gilead.org.il*).

Anderson, Gail-Nina. "Mermaids in Myth and Art," *Fortean Times*, November 2009. (*www.forteantimes.com*).

Ashliman, D. L., PhD. "A Library of Folktales, Folklore, Fairy Tales, and Mythology," University of Pittsburgh. (*www.pitt.edu*).

Bard, Judith. "The Merfolk." (*www.santharia.com*).

Bastian, Misty L. "Nwaanyi Mara Mma: Mami Wata, the More Than Beautiful Woman."

BBC, "Mermaids," (*www.bbc.co.uk*).

Beckwith, Martha Warren, PhD. *Hawaiian Mythology.* (Originally published in 1940; reprinted by BiblioBazaar, 2009).

Blair, Nancy. *Goddesses for Every Season.* (Rockport, MA: Element Books, 2005).

The British Museum. (*www.mesopotamia.co.uk/gods*).

Carlucci, Vincent. "Odd and Interesting Mermaid Facts." (*www.beautiful-mermaid-art.com*)

Cheek, Jonathan, PhD. "The Mermaid Myth," from a course taught at Wellesley College, Wellesley, MA. (*www.wellesley.edu*).

Coghlan, Ronan. *The Illustrated Encyclopaedia of Arthurian Legends.* (Shaftesbury, Dorset: Element Books, 1993).

Conway, D. J. *Magickal Mermaids and Water Creatures.* (Franklin Lakes, NJ: Career Press/New Page Books, 2005).

Cornwall Guide. (*www.cornwalls.co.uk*).

Craig, Robert D. *Dictionary of Polynesian Mythology.* (Westport, CT: Greenwood Press, 1989).

Datz, Margot. *A Survival Guide for Landlocked Mermaids.* (New York: Atria Books, 2008).

Davis, Frederick Hadland. *Myths and Legends of Japan.* (New York: Cosimo, Inc., 2007).

deMason, Scarlett. "Shadows of the Goddess: The Mermaid." (*www.whiterosesgarden.com*).

De Voe, Carrie. *Legends of the Kaw*, Kansas Collection Books.

Drewall, Henry John. *Sacred Waters*. (Bloomington, IN: Indiana University Press, 2008).

Enzler, S. M. "Water Mythology." (*www.lenntech.com/water-mythology.htm*).

Fabian, Johannes. *Remembering the Present: Painting and Popular History in Zaire*. (Berkeley, CA: University of California Press, 1996).

Finnin, Denis. "Mythic Creatures," American Museum of National History. (*www.amnh.org*).

Green, Felicity (ed.). *Togart Contemporary Art Award (NT) 2007*, exhibition catalogue.

Hassam, "Mysterious Myths about Mermaids," (*http://hassam.hubpages.com*).

Hall, Manly P. *The Secret Teachings of All Ages*. (First published 1928, reprinted by Forgotten Books, 2008, *www.sacred-texts.com*).

Jon, Allan Asbjorn. "Dugongs and Mermaids, Selkies and Seals," *Australian Folklore Journal*, No. 13.

Keightley, Thomas. *The Fairy Mythology*. (London: H.G. Bohn, 1870).

Kidd, Sue Monk. *The Mermaid Chair*. (New York: Viking Penguin, 2005).

Kubilius, Kerry. "The Warsaw Mermaid." (*goeasteurope.about.com*).

Lao, Meri. *Seduction and the Secret Power of Women: The Lure of Sirens and Mermaids*. (South Paris, ME: Park Street Press; New Edition of *Sirens: Symbols of Seduction* edition, 2007).

Leach, Maria (ed). *Funk & Wagnall's Standard Dictionary of Folklore, Mythology and Legend*. (New York: Harper & Row, 1984).

Lee, Pali J., and Willis, John K. *Ho'opono-A Night Rainbow Book*. (Honolulu, HI: Native Books, 1999).

Littleton, C. Scott. *Gods, Goddesses, and Mythology, Volume 11*. (Marshall Cavendish Corporation, 2005).

Magic & Mythology: "Fairylore: The Merrow-Folk," (*www.shee-eire.com Magic&Mythology/M&Mmain.htm*).

Marsh, Amy. "A Hidden Meaning of the Mo'o Goddesses." (*waihili.blogspot.com*).

Mayo, Margaret. *Mythical Birds and Beasts from Many Lands*. (New York: Dutton Juvenile, 1997).

Moore, Arthur William. *The Folk-Lore of the Isle of Man*. (Fredonia Books, 2003).

Mysterious Britain & Ireland, (*www.mysteriousbritain.co.uk*).

Mythical Creatures and Beasts, (*www.mythicalcreaturesguide.com*).

The New World Encyclopedia, (*www.newworldencyclopedia.org*).

O'Hanlon, John. *Irish Folklore: Traditions and Superstitions of the Country*. (First published 1870, reprinted by EP Publishing Ltd., Oak Knoll Books, Newcastle, DE, 1973.

Paciorek, Andrew L. "Strange Lands: Supernatural Creatures of the Celtic Otherworld." (*www.batcow.co.uk*).

Piccolo, Anthony, PhD. "Women of the Deep: A Light History of the Mermaid," *Sea History 68*, Winter 1993–4.

Pomare, Maui. *Legends of the Maori.* Part II. "Polynesian History." (New Zealand: Victorian University of Wellington, 2008. *www.nzetc.org*).

Potts, Marc. *The Mythology of the Mermaid and Her Kin.* (Sequim, WA: Holmes Publishing Group, 2001).

Radcliffe-Brown, A.R. "The Rainbow Serpent Myth," *The Journal of the Royal Anthropological Institute of Great Britain and Ireland,* Vol. 56, 1926.

Radford, Patricia. "Lusty Ladies: Mermaids in the Medieval Irish Church," *Insight Magazine.*

Rose, Carol. *Giants, Monsters, and Dragons: An Encyclopedia of Folklore, Legend, and Myth.* (New York: W.W. Norton & Company, 2000).

Siegel, Brian, PhD. "Water Spirits and Mermaids: The Copperbelt Case," paper for Spring 2000 SERSAS Meeting at Western Carolina University, Cullowhee, NC, 2000).

———. "Water Spirits and Mermaids: The Copperbelt *Chitapo*," included in *Sacred Waters*, by Henry John Drewall. (Bloomington, IN: Indiana University Press, 2008, pp. 303–312).

Smith, William, and Stray, Chris. *A Dictionary of Greek and Roman Biography and Mythology.* (London: J. Walton, 1869).

Took, Thalia. *The Goddess Oracle Deck.*

Turnbull, Sharon. *Goddess Gift.* (Quiet Time Press, 2007).

Unknown Explorers, (*www.unknownexplorers.com*).

Valentine, Kathleen. *The Old Mermaid's Tale.* (Gloucester, MA: Parlez-Moi Press, 2007).

———. *The Mermaid's Shawl and Other Beauties.* (Gloucester, MA: Parlez-Moi Press, 2009).

Van Stipriaan, Alex. "Watramama/Mami Wata: Three Centuries of Creolization of a Water Spirit in West Africa, Suriname and Europe," included in *A Pepper-Pot of Cultures: Aspects of Creolization in the Caribbean*, by Gordon Collier (Amsterdam: Editions Rodopi B.V., 2003).

Walker, Barbara G. *The Women's Dictionary of Symbols and Sacred Objects.* (New York: HarperOne, 1988).

Williams, Tom. "Sea's Mysteries: M as in Mermaid or as in Manatee," *Naples Daily News*, September 14, 2008.

www.goodreads.com

www.history.com

www.paleothea.com/Goddesses.html

www.paradoxplace.com

www.tribeofthesun.com

Zogbé, Mama. "Mami Wata: From Myth to Divine Reality." (*www.mamiwata.com*).

Index

About the Author

SKYE ALEXANDER is the award-winning author of more than thirty fiction and nonfiction books. Her stories have been published in anthologies internationally, and her work has been translated into more than a dozen languages. She is also an artist with a special interest in mythical and metaphysical subjects. She divides her time between Texas and Massachusetts. She invites you to visit her website and blog (*www.skyealexander.com*).